THE TRIPODS

THE CITY OF GOLD AND LEAD

Also by John Christopher

The White Mountains
The Pool of Fire
When the Tripods Came
A Dusk of Demons

THE TRIPODS

THE CITY OF
GOLD AND LEAD

JOHN CHRISTOPHER

Simon Pulse
New York   London   Toronto   Sydney

To Rose, Liz, and Nick,
with love

First Aladdin Paperbacks edition, 1970
Second Aladdin Paperbacks edition, 1988
Revised cover edition, 1999
First Simon Pulse edition, April 2003
Text copyright © 1967 by John Christopher

SIMON PULSE
An imprint of Simon & Schuster Children's Publishing Division
1230 Avenue of the Americas, New York, NY 10020

Design by Ann Sullivan
The text of this book was set in New Caledonia.
Manufactured in the United States of America
20 19 18 17 16 15 14 13

The Library of Congress has cataloged the hardcover edition as follows:
Christopher, John.
City of Gold and Lead / John Christopher.
p. cm.
Sequel to: The white mountains.
Sequel: the pool of fire.
Summary: Three boys set out on a secret mission to penetrate the City of the Tripods and learn more about these strange beings that rule the earth.
[1. Science fiction.] I. Title PZ7.C457 Ci 2003 [Fic]—dc21
2002026670
ISBN-13: 978-0-689-85666-2 (pbk.)
ISBN-10: 0-689-85666-0 (pbk.)

Contents

Preface

Writers are borrowers and thieves. Computer analysis has recently revealed that the best of us all, William Shakespeare, based two of his early plays on works by his then more distinguished contemporary, Christopher Marlowe. Because he *was* Shakespeare, his versions turned out far better than anything Marlowe could have achieved. And as Shakespeare's genius matured, he no longer had a need to borrow; other writers borrowed from him instead.

It wasn't quite like that in my own case: I stole from a much better writer than myself. All I can offer by way of extenuation is a) I didn't know I was doing it and b) I did my best to add a little something of my own.

I'd written *The White Mountains* in a spirit of venturing into new and uncharted territory. I was far from sure it would prove acceptable, even to the English publisher who'd asked me to write it; let alone to a wider audience. I also realized that, if it was approved, I was going to be leaving loose ends which would need another book to sort out, although I had no notion of having embarked on a trilogy.

The chief loose end lay in the nature of the Tripods: Were they intelligent machines, or awe-inspiring carriers of mysterious aliens? I had actually used Tripods before in an adult science fiction story (thankfully forgotten), without even wondering where I'd got them from. I now realized where I'd picked up the idea: H. G. Wells' *The War of the Worlds.*

This was an almost incredible example of amnesia. As a boy, I had been fanatically devoted to science fiction—principally through the medium of American pulp magazines, but I had also worshipfully devoured all the scientific romances of the great H. G. Wells, of which *The War of the Worlds* is among the most notable. And possibly the most famous: in the thirties Orson Welles made extraordinary use of the book to terrify radio listeners across a large tract of North America into thinking the story was real.

If I *had* understood the source of the Tripods earlier, I would never, of course, have used such a device; but with *The White Mountains* finished and on its way to publication, I realized I was stuck with the borrowing. So I started trying to make it my own.

On the face of things, tripods do not seem a particularly sensible way of getting around.

They are large and they stand awesomely tall, but they're clumsy and relatively slow-moving as well. I thought about my illustrious predecessor, and realized that he too had been struck by the visual image—undeniably a powerful one—but had not given much thought to more practical considerations. His tripods had been vehicles for intelligent, spiderlike Martians. But why on earth would an arachnid species use something so improbable, and so impractical? They would have done better, for instance, if they had replicated their own body structure and deployed eight-legged, crawler-type vehicles in their invasion of planet Earth.

And why would they develop these stiltlike vehicles on a planet which astronomers had assured us was desertlike and largely flat? It made no sense. But then I recalled that there had been something that was reminiscent of Tripods in our own history: the stilt men of Landes.

Landes is a region of southwest France fronting the Bay of Biscay, now drained and cultivated but before the nineteenth century a marsh-filled swampy region. Sheep grazed there on the hummocks of grassland between the swamps, and their shepherds needed a better way of looking after them than by trudging around in the muddy wetlands. So they developed stilts, on which they could stalk about tending their flocks, carrying long sticks to reach down to the ground below (the third leg of the Tripod?). Even today, at the town of Dax, famous for its mineral springs, there are annual demonstrations of stilting—not just walking on stilts, but dancing and engaging in sporting events. Stilt walking was also developed in Belgium, and in the Marquesas islands in the South Pacific.

So perhaps, I speculated, these aliens had come from a swampy planet. And perhaps, unlike Wells' Martians, they *had* been into the idea of body replication. They had invented Tripods rather than stilts . . . because they themselves were three-legged? I was beginning to get a grip on things.

How would a Tripod move—which leg went first, and which followed? Try it yourself, walking three fingers across a table: it isn't easy. And it was a question that cropped up seriously in 1983 when the BBC made a television series based on the books. The producer, Richard Bates, put the problem to me, and I airily told him not to worry. A revival of the MGM movie based on Wells' book was to be shown on television the following week; all we had to do was watch that, and find out. But when we did, we found that the film producers had chickened out of the difficulty— instead of tripods they featured flying capsules, supported by invisible force beams. So I handed on the problem to Arthur C. Clarke (before he became Sir Arthur). He said that while it was indeed difficult, there should be a solution, but it would be a pretty abstract one, involving the utilization of higher mathematics.

Daunted by this, I went back and took another look at *The White Mountains,* only to find that I'd actually already worked it out for myself but forgotten about it. The only reasonable means of progress for a Tripod is by way of a twirling motion, a kind of spiraling advance. So if Tripods twirled, maybe so did the three-legged Masters. And perhaps they had three eyes, to take in a continuously shifting perspective—two more steps on the road to getting things right.

Coming from a hot steamy planet, the aliens would want to maintain a similar environment in their citadel strongholds on Earth. In addition, the massive scale of the Tripods suggested that their planet was larger than ours, with a higher gravitational force—they would need to reproduce that, too. I was beginning to envisage what their headquarters might look like: a walled, domed city with a gleaming gold exterior and an artificial gravity within that would relentlessly wear down any humans brought inside. A city of gold and lead.

—**John Christopher, 2003**

THE TRIPODS

THE CITY OF
GOLD AND LEAD

One

Three Are Chosen

Even when we first came to the White Mountains, in summer, the upper reaches of the Tunnel looked out over fields of snow and ice; but at the lower end there were rocks and grass and a view of the glacier, stained brown with mud and dripping into rivulets that ran down to the valley, far far below. In September there was a fall of snow which did not lie, but in the early days of October the snow came again, more heavily, and this time remained. The grip of winter tightened around us, and it was to be more than half a year before those white bony fingers unclenched.

Preparations for the siege had been made

long before. Food had been stored, cattle and winter fodder taken into the inner recesses of the mountain which sheltered us. We did not need a great deal by way of heat, protected as we were by dozens, hundreds of yards of solid rock. Cool in summer, our deep caves were warm, by comparison, in winter. We wore furs when we were outside, but the rest of the time our normal clothing was enough.

Our lives were confined, but by no means idle. Reveille, for those of us in the training cadre, was at six, and was followed by half an hour's brisk exercise. After that came a simple breakfast, and then the first study period of the day, lasting three hours. There were more exercises before the midday meal, and in the afternoon exercise and instruction in our particular sports. If the weather were fine, this took place outside in the snow; otherwise in the Great Cavern. There was a second study period before supper, and afterward generally there was discussion among our seniors, to which we listened but in which we did not presume to join. It had one subject—the Tripods—and one purpose: their overthrow.

The Tripods had been rulers of the earth for more than a hundred years. They governed simply and effectively, by dominating the minds of men. This was achieved through the Caps, meshes of silvery metal which fitted closely around the skull and were woven into the very flesh of their wearers. Capping occurred in one's fourteenth year, marking the point at which one ceased to be a child and became an adult. It was taken for granted, an expected, looked-for thing, attended by feasting and celebration.

A few months earlier I had seen my cousin Jack, a year older than myself, go through the ceremony, and had noticed the change in him afterward. I was to be Capped the following year. I had some misgivings, but I kept them private—no one talked much about Tripods and Cappings and, of course, no one ever queried the rightness of these things. Not, that is, until the Vagrant, Ozymandias, came to the little village where I lived.

The Vagrants were those for whom Capping had not worked properly. Their minds had refused to accept the conditioning of the Tripods and, in refusing, had been broken. They wandered from place to place, never resting long, and were looked after but pitied and disliked by normal Capped men and women. Now, though, I found myself more interested in them; particularly in the one who called himself Ozymandias, a big, red-haired, red-bearded man who sang strange songs, and spoke lines of poetry, and mixed sense and nonsense when he talked. Defying my parents, I invited him to come to the den which Jack and I had made just outside the village. He told me a strange story.

He was, in the first place, not really a Vagrant, but posing as such so that he could travel through the land, unchallenged and unremarked. The Cap he wore was a false one. He explained that the Tripods were enemies of men, not benefactors, invaders, perhaps, from another world, and how, through Capping, minds which were just beginning to think for themselves were subdued and harnessed to the worship of their oppressors. He told me, too, that although the Tripods ruled the planet, there were a few places where free men survived, and that one of these was among the White Mountains, across the sea from England far to the south. He asked me if I would be willing to make a difficult and dangerous journey there, and I said I would.

He himself traveled on in search of more recruits, but I did not go alone. Another cousin of mine, Henry, an old antagonist since before our schooldays, saw me leaving the village and followed me. We crossed the sea together, and in the land called France found a third, Jean-Paul—whom we named Beanpole. Together we made our way south. It was as difficult and dangerous as Ozymandias had promised. Near the end, we fought a battle with a Tripod and, by luck and a weapon of the ancients which we found in the ruins of one of the great-cities, destroyed it.

So, at last, we reached the White Mountains.

•••

There were eleven of us in the training cadre, being prepared for the first move in the counterattack against our enemies. It was a hard schooling, in body and mind alike, but we knew a little of the task before us, and how heavy the odds against success were. The discipline and hardship we had to endure might not shorten those odds by much, but every bit counted.

For we—or some of us—were to conduct a reconnaissance. We knew almost nothing of the Tripods—not even whether they were intelligent machines or vehicles for alien beings. We must know more before we could hope to fight them successfully; and there was only one way to get that knowledge. Some of us, one at least, must penetrate into the City of the Tripods, study them, and bring back information. The plan was this:

The City lay to the north, in the country of the Germans. Each year some of the newly Capped, chosen in different ways, were brought there to serve the Tripods. I had witnessed one such way at the Château de la Tour Rouge, when Eloise, the daughter of the Comte, had been made Queen of the Tournament. I had been horrified to learn that at the end of her brief reign she should want to be taken to be a slave of the enemy, and go gladly, thinking it an honor.

Among the Germans, it seemed, there were

Games each summer, to which young men came from hundreds of miles away. The winners were feasted and made much of after which they, too, went to serve in the City. At the next Games, it was hoped, one of us might win, and gain admission. What would happen after that was unknown. Anyone who succeeded would have to rely on his wits, both in spying on the Tripods and in passing on what he had learned. The last part was likely to be the hardest. Because although scores, perhaps hundreds, went yearly into the City, not one had ever been known to come out.

One day the snow was melting at the foot of the Tunnel where we exercised, and a week later it lay only in isolated patches, and there was the green of grass, dotted with purple crocuses. The sky was blue, and sunlight flamed from the white peaks all round, burning our skins through the thin pure air. During a break we lay on the grass and looked down. Figures moved cautiously half a mile below, visible to us but taking cover from those who might look up from the valley. This was the first raiding party of the season, on its way to plunder the fat lands of the Capped.

I sat with Henry and Beanpole, a little apart from the rest. The lives of all those who lived in the mountains were closely knit, but this strand was a more tightly woven one. In the things we had endured, jealousies and enmities had worn away and been replaced by true comradeship. The boys in the cadre were our friends, but the bond between us three was special.

Beanpole said gloomily, "I failed at one meter seventy today."

He spoke in German; we had learned the language but needed to practice it. I said, "One goes off form. You'll improve again."

"I'm getting worse every day."

Henry said, "Rodrigo's definitely gone off. I beat him comfortably."

"It's all right for you."

Henry had been chosen as a long-distance runner, and Rodrigo was his chief rival. Beanpole was training for long and high jumping. I was one of two boxers. There were four sports altogether—the other was sprint running—and they had been arranged to produce a maximum of competitiveness. Henry had done well in his event from the start. And I myself was fairly confident, at any rate, as far as my opponent here was concerned. This was Tonio, a dark-skinned boy from the south, taller than I and with a longer reach, but not as quick. Beanpole, though, had grown increasingly pessimistic about his chances.

Henry reassured him, telling him he had heard the instructors saying he was coming on well. I wondered if it were true, or said for encouragement: the former, I hoped.

I said, "I asked Johann if it had been decided yet how many were to go."

Johann, one of the instructors, was squat and powerful, yellow-haired, with the look of a bad-tempered bull but amiable at heart. Henry asked, "What did he say?"

"He wasn't sure, but he thought four—the best from each group."

"So it could be us three, plus an extra," Henry said.

Beanpole shook his head. "I'll never do it."

"You will."

I said, "And the fourth?"

"It might be Fritz."

He did seem to be the best of the sprint runners, as far as we could tell. He was German himself, and came from a place on the edge of a forest to the northeast. His chief rival was a French boy, Etienne, whom I preferred. Etienne was cheerful and talkative, Fritz tall, heavy, taciturn.

I said, "As long as we all come through."

"You two will," Beanpole said.

Henry leaped to his feet. "There's the whistle. Come on, Beanpole. Time to get back to work."

The seniors had their own tasks. Some were our instructors; others formed the raiding parties to keep us supplied with food. There were still others who studied the few books that had survived from olden days, and tried to relearn the skills and mysteries of our ancestors. Beanpole, whenever he had a chance, would be with them, listening to their talk and even putting up suggestions of his own. Not long after we met he had spoken—wildly, as I thought—about using a sort of gigantic kettle to push carriages without the need for horses. Something like this had been discovered, or rediscovered, here, though it would not yet work properly. And there were plans for more remarkable things: making light and heat through something which had been called electricity was one.

And at the head of all the groups there was one man, whose hands held all the threads, whose decisions were unquestioned. This was Julius.

He was close on sixty years old, a small man and a cripple. When he was a boy he had fallen into an ice crevasse and broken his thigh: it had been set badly and he walked with a limp. In those days, things had been very different in the White Mountains. Those who lived there had no purpose but survival, and their numbers were dwindling. It was Julius who thought of winning recruits from the world outside, from those not yet Capped, and who believed—and made others believe—that some day men would fight back against the Tripods, and destroy them.

It was Julius, too, who had worked out the enterprise for which we were being trained. And it was Julius who would make the final decision on which of us were chosen.

He came out one day to watch us. He was white-haired, red-cheeked like most of those who had lived all their lives in this sharp, clear air, and he leaned on a stick. I saw him, and concentrated hard on the bout in which I was engaged. Tonio feinted with his left, and followed up with a right cross. I made him miss, hammered a sharp right to his ribs and, when he came in again, landed a left to the jaw which sent him sprawling.

Julius beckoned, and I ran to where he stood. He said, "You are improving, Will."

"Thank you, sir."

"I suppose you are getting impatient to know which of you will be going to the Games?"

I nodded. "A little, sir."

He studied me. "When the Tripod had you in its grasp—do you remember how you felt? Were you afraid?"

I remembered. I said, "Yes, sir."

"And the thought of being in their hands, in their City—does that frighten you?" I hesitated, and he went on: "There are two sides to the choice, you know. We old ones may be able to judge your quickness and skill, of mind and body, but we cannot read your hearts."

"Yes," I admitted, "it frightens me."

"You do not have to go. You can be useful here." His pale blue eyes looked into mine. "No one need know if you prefer to stay."

I said, "I want to go. I can bear the thought of being in their hands more easily than of being left behind."

"Good." He smiled. "And you, after all, have killed a Tripod—something I doubt any other human being can claim. You know that they are not all-powerful. That is an asset, Will."

"Do you mean, sir . . . ?"

"I mean what I said. There are other considerations. You must go on working hard, and preparing, in case you are chosen."

Later I saw him talking to Henry. I thought it was probably much the same conversation as mine had been. I did not ask him, though, and he did not volunteer anything about it.

During the winter our diet, although adequate, had been very dull, the staple item dried and salted meat, which, however hard the cooks tried, remained stodgy and unappetizing. In the middle of April, though, a raiding party brought back half a dozen black-and-white cows, and Julius decreed that one should be killed and roasted. After the feast, he spoke to us. When he had been talking a few minutes I realized, the excitement almost suffocating me, that this, almost certainly, was the moment for announcing the names of those who were to make the attempt at penetrating the City of the Tripods.

He had a quiet voice, and I was with the other boys at the far end of the cave, but his words were clear. Everyone was listening, attentively and in silence. I glanced at Henry, on my right. In the flickering light, I thought he looked very confident. My own confidence was ebbing rapidly. It would be bitter if he went, and I were left.

First, Julius talked about the plan in general. For months those in the training cadre had been preparing for their task. They would have some advantage over competitors from lower lands, because it was known that men in higher altitudes developed stronger lungs and muscles than those who lived in the thicker air. But it had to be remembered that there would be hundreds of competitors, drawn from the best athletes all over the country. It might be that, for all their preparation, not one of our small band would wear a champion's belt. In that case, they must find their way back to the White Mountains, and try again, next year. Patience was as necessary as determination.

Contestants in the Games must be Capped, of course. That presented no great difficulty. We had Caps, taken from those killed in forays into the valleys, which could be molded to fit the skulls of the ones chosen. They would look like Caps, but they would give no orders. Here, though, a problem did present itself.

We who had never been Capped could not know just how men's minds were controlled by them. It might be that they simply fixed the wearers in an attitude of uncritical obedience, of devotion, to the Tripods. In that case, our spies only needed to put on the appearance of willing slaves. But there was the possibility that the Tripods could talk to the minds of the Capped through the Caps, without the need for speech. That, it was plain, would mean discovery, and either execution or Capping. The former was the better fate.

Not only for the individuals but for those who stayed behind. It had been objected—I wondered who had dared to object to a plan put forward by Julius—that this involved the risk of betraying our existence to the Tripods, of provoking them to bring their power to bear and crush us. The risk must be taken. We could not skulk forever in the mountains. Even if we hid in holes all the time, eventually they would ferret us out and exterminate us, like vermin. Our hope of survival lay in attack.

Now to the details of the plan:

The City of the Tripods lay hundreds of miles to the north. There was a great river which covered most of that distance. Barges plied up and down it in trade, and one of these was in the hands of our men. It would sail to a spot within easy reach of the place where the Games were held.

Julius paused, before going on.

It had been decided that three should be selected from the training cadre. Many things had to be taken into account: individual skill and strength, the likely level of competition in the event, the temperament of the person and his probable usefulness once he had penetrated the Tripods' stronghold. It had not been easy, but the choices had been made. Raising his voice slightly, he called.

"Stand up, Will Parker."

For all my hopes, the shock of hearing my own name unnerved me. My legs trembled as I got to my feet.

Julius said, "You have shown ability as a boxer, Will, and you have the advantage of being small and light in weight. Your training has been with Tonio, who would be in a heavier class at the Games, and this should help you.

"The doubt we had was about you yourself. You are impatient, often thoughtless, likely to rush into things without giving careful enough consideration to what may happen next. From that point of view, Tonio would have been better. But he is less likely to succeed at the Games, which is our first concern. A heavy responsibility may rest on you. Can we rely on you to do your utmost to guard against your own recklessness?"

I promised, "Yes, sir."

"Sit down, then, Will. Stand up, Jean-Paul Deliet."

I think I felt gladder about Beanpole than when my own name was called; perhaps because I was less confused and had been less optimistic. I had picked up his own gloom about his chances. So there would be three—the three of us who had journeyed together before, who had fought the Tripod on the hillside.

Julius said, "There were difficulties in your case, too, Jean-Paul. You are the best of our jumpers, but it is not sure that you are up to the standard that will be necessary to win at the Games. And there is the question of your eyesight. The contraption of lenses you invented— or rediscovered because they were common among the ancients—is something that passed as an eccentricity in a boy, but the Capped do not have such eccentricities. You must blunder through a world in which you will see less clearly than your fellows. If you get inside the City, you will not perceive things with the clarity that Will, for instance, would.

"But what you see, you may understand better. Your intelligence is an asset which outweighs the weakness of your eyes. You could be the most useful in bringing back to us what we have to know. Do you accept the task?"

Beanpole said, "Yes, sir."

"And so we come to the third choice, which was the easiest." I saw Henry looking pleased with himself, and was childish enough to feel a little resentment. "He is the most likely to succeed in his event, and the best equipped for what may follow.

"Fritz Eger—do you accept?"

I tried to speak to Henry, but he made it plain that he wanted to be left alone. I saw him again later on, but he was morose and uncommunicative. Then, the following morning, I happened to go to the lookout gallery, and found him there.

The main Tunnel had been built by the ancients to take horseless carriages up through the mountain to a point near the top, where the great glacier rolled away between snowy peaks to the southeast. We had no idea why they had done that, but there was a big house at the top, and a building with a domed roof of metal that had a vast telescope pointing at the sky, and a cave where strange figures were carved in ice. On the way up, there were galleries, from which one looked out and down, and the lowest of these showed a rich green valley, thousands of feet below, in which one could see roads like black thread, tiny houses, pinpoint cattle in miniature meadows. There was a telescope here, too, a small one fixed in the rock, but one of the lenses had been broken and it was useless.

Henry was leaning against the low wall of rock, and turned as I approached. I said awkwardly, "If you want me to go . . ."

"No." He shrugged. "It doesn't matter."

"I'm . . . sorry."

He managed a grin. "Not as sorry as I am."

"If we went to see Julius . . . I don't see why there shouldn't be four instead of three."

"I've already seen him."

"And there's no hope?"

"None. I'm the best of my group, but they don't think I'd stand much chance in the Games. Perhaps next year, if I keep at it."

"I don't see why you shouldn't *try* this year."

"I said that, too. He says even three is really too large a party to send out. So much more chance of being spotted, and more difficult with the barge."

One did not argue with Julius. I said, "Well, you will have a chance next year."

"If there is a next year."

There would only be a second expedition if this one failed. I thought of what failure could mean, to me personally. The diminutive valley of fields and houses and ribboned rivers, on which I had so often looked with longing, was as sunny as before, but suddenly less attractive. I was staring at it from a dark hole, but one in which I had come to feel safe.

Yet even in the brush of fear, I felt sorry for Henry. I could have been the one left behind. I did not think I would have borne it as well, if so.

Two

Prisoner in the Pit

We set out in late afternoon, made our way secretly through the nearer valleys during dusk, and traveled on by moonlight. We did not rest until the sun was high, and by then we were halfway along the shore of the westerly of the twin lakes that lay below our stronghold. We hid ourselves on the hillside: behind and far above us was the glistening white peak from which we had started our journey. We were tired. We ate, and then slept, exhausted, through the long hot day.

It was a hundred miles to the point on the river at which we were to join the *Erlkönig*. We had a guide—one of the men who knew the country from raiding parties—who would go with us as far as the barge. We went mostly by night, lying up during the daylight hours.

This was some weeks after the feast, and Julius's announcement. During that time we had been given further instruction and preparation, starting with having our hair cropped short and the false Cap molded to fit close to our skulls. It had been strange and desperately uncomfortable at first, but gradually I had grown used to this hard helmet of metal. My hair was already growing through and around the mesh, and we were assured that before the Games began we should look no different from other boys who had been Capped, as they generally were there, in the first weeks of summer. At night we wore bonnets of wool, because otherwise the cold would strike through the metal, painfully waking us.

Henry had not been among those who watched us leave the Tunnel. I understood that: I would not have wanted to be there if our situations had been reversed. My impulse was to resent Fritz, who had taken his place, but I remembered what Julius had said about needing to curb my rashness. I remembered also that I had resented what I thought was the greater friendship between Beanpole and Henry on our journey south, and how I had allowed it to influence me during our stay at the Château de la Tour Rouge.

I determined not to let anything of that kind happen now, and with this in mind made a special effort to be nice to him. But there was a poor response to my overtures; Fritz remained taciturn and withdrawn. I was prepared to resent that, in turn, but succeeded in bottling up my annoyance. It was a great help that Beanpole was with us. He and I did most of the talking, when we were in circumstances where talking did not involve risk. Our guide, Primo, a dark burly man, looking clumsy but in fact wonderfully sure-footed, said little beyond what was necessary by way of warning and instruction.

A week had been allowed, but we covered the distance in four days. We followed a high ridge, skirting the ruins of one of the great-cities. These encompassed a bend in the river which was to be our thoroughfare. It came from the east, with the early morning sun glinting along its length, but here turned and flowed northward. The higher stretch was empty, as was the part that ran between the sullen humps that had once been towering buildings, but above that there was traffic—two barges nosing downriver, perhaps a dozen tied up by the bank, at the wharves of a small town.

Primo pointed down.

"One of those will be the *Erlkönig*. You can find your way down there on your own?"

We assured him that we could.

"Then I'll be getting back." He nodded briefly. "Good luck to you."

• • •

The *Erlkönig* was one of the smaller barges, and some fifty feet in length. There was nothing special about her; she was just a long low structure rising a few feet above the surface of the water, with a partly covered wheelhouse aft, giving the steersman some protection against the elements. She had a crew of two, both false-Capped. The senior of these was called Ulf, a squat, barrel-chested man in his forties, with a brusque manner and a habit of punctuating his speech by spitting. I did not like him, the more so after he had made a disparaging remark about my slightness of build. His companion, Moritz, was about ten years younger and, I thought, ten times pleasanter. He had fair hair, a thin face, and a warm and ready smile. But there could be no doubt as to which of them was master: Moritz deferred to Ulf automatically. And it was Ulf, spitting and grunting at regular intervals, who gave us our instructions for the voyage.

"We're a two-man barge," he told us. "An extra boy is fair enough—you start 'prentices that way. But any more would draw notice, and I'm not having it. So you'll take it in turns to work on deck—and when I say work, boy, I mean it— and the other two will lie below decks and won't come up even if she's foundering. You've been told the need for discipline, I take it, so I don't have to go into that. All I want to say is this: I shall give short shrift to anyone who causes trouble, for whatever reason.

"I know the job you've got to do, and I hope you're up to it. But if you can't behave sensibly and obey orders on this trip, you're not likely to be any good later on. So I won't think twice about dropping somebody off who's out of line. And since I wouldn't want him to float into the wrong harbor and start people asking questions, I've got a weight of iron to tie on his legs before I do drop him off."

He cleared his throat, spat and growled. The last remark, I thought, was possibly meant to be a joke. But I was not sure. He looked capable of carrying out the threat.

He went on, "You've arrived early, which is better than arriving late. It'll take a day to load cargo, but we're not due off for another three. We can leave a day early, but no more. So the first couple below have a two-day stint before they see the sky. Do you want to draw lots for it?"

I glanced at Beanpole. Two days on deck were vastly preferable to spending the time below. But there was the possibility of two days confined with the silent Fritz. Beanpole, his mind presumably working along the same lines, said, "Will and I will volunteer to stay below."

Ulf looked at me, and I nodded. He said, "Just as you like. Show them where they can bunk, Moritz."

A problem that had engaged Beanpole as we came down from the hill to the river bank had been the way in which the barges were propelled. They had no sails, and these, in any case, would have been of limited value in the confines of a river. They could go down, of course, easily enough with the current, but how had they come up to this point, against it? As we got nearer, we saw that the barges had paddle wheels in their sides, and Beanpole was excited by the thought that there might be some machine, surviving from the days of the ancients, which moved them.

The truth was disappointing. Each wheel had a treadmill inside, and the treadmill, on journeys upriver, was worked by donkeys. Trained for the task when young, they strained steadily forward and their exertions pulled the barge through the water. It seemed a hard and dreary life, and I was sorry for them, but they were well looked after by Moritz, who was plainly fond of the beasts. They were worked very little on the downriver trips, and were pastured out whenever there was an opportunity. They were in a field not far from the river bank now, and would stay there till it was time for the *Erlkönig* to move. Until they came aboard, Beanpole and I stayed in their small stables, with the smell of donkey and fodder mixing with the smells of old cargoes.

The cargo this time was of wooden clocks and carvings. The people who lived in the great forest east of the river made these, and they were shipped downriver to be sold. They had to be loaded with care because of their fragility, and men came aboard the barge to see to this. Beanpole and I hid behind the bales of hay which were kept for the donkeys and did our best to stay quiet. Once I could not stop myself sneezing, but luckily they were talking and laughing loudly enough not to hear it.

But it was a relief when the two days were up and, in the early morning, the barge cast off and moved out into the river. The donkeys worked their treadmill—two at a time with one resting— and Beanpole and I drew straws for who was to take Fritz's place on deck. I won, and went up to a dark blowy day, with a wind from the north that carried occasional gusts of rain. The air was wonderfully sweet and fresh after my confinement, and there were many interesting things to be seen, both on the river and around it. Westward there was a great fertile plain, with people working in the fields. To the east the hills stood up, with the black clouds pressing down over their wooded crests. I did not have much time, though, to admire the scenery. Ulf called me and made me get a bucket of water, a brush, and a handful of yellow soft soap. The decks, he observed truthfully enough, had not been scrubbed for some weeks. I could make myself useful by remedying that.

The progress of the *Erlkönig* was steady, but not fast. In the evening, before it was dark, we tied up on a long island where another barge was already moored. This was one of a number of staging posts that apparently ran the five-hundred-mile length of the river. Moritz explained to me that they were set a distance apart, which was calculated as a minimum day's haul upriver. Going down with the current, one usually covered two stages easily in a day, but to achieve a third meant risking darkness falling before one got there. The barges did not travel by night.

We had seen no sign of Tripods during our journey from the White Mountains, through the valleys, to the river. During this day on deck, I saw two. Both were distant, striding along the western skyline, three or four miles away at least. But the sight of them gave me a shiver of fear, which took some subduing. For quite long periods it was possible to forget the exact nature of the mission on which we had embarked. Being reminded of it was a nasty jolt.

I tried to console myself with the thought that there had been no hitches so far, that everything was going well. It did not help much, but by the following evening even that small consolation had gone.

The *Erlkönig* stopped at the halfway stage. This was in a small town, a trading post. Moritz explained that Ulf had some business to conduct there. It would only take him an hour or so, but he had decided, since we were in advance of schedule, to stay over until the following morning. The afternoon lengthened, though, and there was no sign of Ulf returning. Moritz became more and more visibly nervous.

In the end he voiced his apprehensions. Ulf, it seemed, was a man who drank heavily on occasion. Moritz had thought he would not do so on this trip, in view of everything that hung on it, but if the business on which he was engaged had gone wrong and he had become irritated by that, he might have stopped at a tavern, intending to have a drink to soothe his temper, and one thing might have led to another . . . In a bad bout he might be away from the barge several days.

This was a discouraging thought. The sun dropped down in the west, and there was no Ulf. Moritz began to talk of leaving us on the barge and going in search of him.

The difficulty was that the *Erlkönig,* and Ulf and Moritz, were well known in this town. Already a couple of men had stopped by, to offer greetings, and chat for a while. If Moritz left, Beanpole would have to handle them (it was his day on deck), and Moritz was unhappy about that. Suspicions might be aroused. They were likely to quiz him in his role as a new apprentice—people on the river were curious about strangers, knowing each other so well—and he might be led into saying something which they would recognize as false.

It was Beanpole who suggested another way. We boys could go and look for Ulf. Choosing moments when no eye was watching, we could slip away in turn, and hunt around the taverns till we found him; then either persuade him to return or, at least, tell Moritz where he was. If we were questioned, we could pass as travelers from far parts: after all, the town was a trading post. It was not the same as having to answer questions about what we were doing on board the *Erlkönig*.

Moritz was dubious, but admitted there was some point in this. Gradually he allowed himself to be persuaded. It was out of the question for all three of us to go searching for Ulf, but one might—Beanpole, since it had been his idea. So Beanpole went, and I at once started working on Moritz to let me go also.

I was helped by the fact that my importunity was matched, on Fritz's part, by indifference. He made no comment and clearly was prepared to wait until things sorted themselves out without assistance from him. So, having allowed one to go, there was only one other for Moritz to consider. I wore him down, as I had known I would; he was more amiable than Ulf, much more amiable, but also less sure of himself. He insisted that

I should be back within the hour, whether or not I found Ulf, and I agreed to that. I was tingling with the excitement of exploring a strange town, in a strange country. I checked that no one was watching the barge, then jumped quickly onto the quay and made my way along the waterfront.

The town was a bigger place than I had thought, looking at it from the deck of the barge. Fronting the river there was a row of warehouses and granaries, many of them with three floors above the ground. The buildings were partly of stone but principally of wood, which was carved and painted with figures of men and animals. There were a couple of taverns in this stretch, and I looked in briefly though Beanpole, I guessed, would have covered these before me. One of them was empty, except for two old men, sitting with large mugs of beer (they were called *steins*, I knew) and smoking pipes. The other had perhaps a dozen men in it, but I could tell in a quick survey that none of them was Ulf.

I came to a road, running at right angles to the river, and followed it. There were shops here, and a fair amount of horse traffic, with pony traps and larger carriages and men on horseback. There were, I thought, a lot of people about. I understood why on coming to the first intersection. The crossing road, in either direction, was blocked by stalls, selling food and cloth and all kinds of goods. It was market day.

It was exhilarating, after the long winter of exercise and study, in the darkness of the Tunnel or on the bareness of the mountainside, to be once more among people going about their daily lives. And particularly exhilarating for me, who before fleeing to the White Mountains had known only the quietness of a country village. A few times I had been taken to Winchester for the market there, and had marveled at it. This town seemed to be as big as Winchester—perhaps even bigger.

I made my way past the stalls. The first was piled high with vegetables—carrots and little potatoes, fat green-and-white spears of asparagus, peas and huge cabbages, both green and red. At the next there was meat—not simple cuts such as the butcher brought to my village in England; but joints and chops and rolls delicately decorated with dabs of white lard. I wandered along, gazing and sniffing. A stall was completely given over to cheeses, of a score of different colors, shapes, and sizes. I had not realized there could be so many. And there was a fish stall, with dried and smoked fish hanging from hooks and fish fresh caught from the river laid out along a stone slab, their scales still wet. Now, with the dusk gathering, some of the stalls were preparing to close down but most were busy yet, and the stream of people, threading their way between and past them was thick enough.

Between two stalls, one selling leather and the other bolts of cloth, I saw the opening to a tavern, and guiltily remembered what I was supposed to be doing. I went inside, and looked about me. It was darker than the taverns on the waterfront, full of tobacco smoke and crowded with dim figures, some sitting at tables and others standing by the bar counter. As I went up to look more closely, I was addressed from the other side of the bar. The speaker was a very big, very fat man, wearing a leather jacket with sleeves of green cloth. In a rough voice, with an accent that I could barely understand, he said, "What is it, then, lad?"

Moritz had given me some coins of the money used in these parts. I did what seemed the safest thing, and ordered a *Dunkles*, which I knew to be the name of the dark ale that was commonly drunk. The *stein* was larger than I had expected. He brought it to me, with ale foaming over the side, and I gave him a coin. I drank, and had to wipe foam from my lips. It had a bittersweet taste, which was not unpleasant. I looked around for Ulf, peering into the many dark recesses, whose paneled walls carried the mounted heads of deer and wild boar. I thought for a moment I saw him, but the man moved into the light of an oil lamp, and was a stranger.

I felt nervous. Having a Cap I was, of course, counted as a man now, so there was no reason why I should not be here. But I lacked the assurance of someone who had been truly Capped and was aware, of course, of my difference from all these others. Having established that Ulf was not one of the figures sprawling at the tables, I was eager to be away. As inconspicuously as possible, I put the *stein* down and began to move toward the street. Before I had gone a couple of paces, the man in the leather jacket roared at me, and I turned back.

"Here!" He pushed over some smaller coins. "You're forgetting your change."

I thanked him, and once more prepared to go. By this time, though, he had seen the *stein*, and that it was two-thirds full.

"You've not drunk your ale, either. Are you saying it's a poor brew?"

I hastily said no, that it was just that I was not feeling well. To my dismay, I realized that others were taking an interest in me. The man behind the bar seemed partly mollified, but said, "You're not a Württemberger, by the way you talk. Where are you from, then?"

This was a challenge for which I had been prepared. We were to hail from outlying places, in my case a land to the south called Tirol. I told him this.

As far as allaying suspicion was concerned, it worked.

From another point of view, though, it was an

unfortunate choice. I learned later that there was strong feeling in the town against the Tirol. The previous year at the Games a local champion had been defeated by a Tiroler and, it was claimed, through trickery. One of the others standing by now asked if I were going to the Games, and I incautiously said yes. What followed was a stream of insults. Tirolers were cheats and braggarts, and they spurned good Württemberg ale. They ought to be run out of town, dipped in the river to clean them up a bit . . .

The thing to do was to get out, and fast. I stomached the insults and turned to go. Once outside I could lose myself in the crowd. I was thinking of that and did not look closely enough in front of me. A leg was stretched out from one of the tables and, to the accompaniment of a roar of laughter, I went sprawling in the sawdust that covered the floor.

Even that I was prepared to endure, though I had banged one knee painfully as I landed. I began to get to my feet. As I did so, fingers gripped the hair that grew up through my Cap, and shook my head violently to and fro, and thrust me down once more to the ground.

I should have been thankful that this assault had not dislodged the false Cap and exposed me. I should also have been concentrating on what really mattered—getting away from here and safely and unnoticed back to the barge. But I am afraid that I could think of nothing but the pain and humiliation. I got up again, saw a face grinning behind me, and swung at him in fury.

He was probably a year or so older than I was, and bigger and heavier. He fended me off contemptuously. My mind did not cool down enough for me to realize how stupidly I was behaving, but enough for the skills I had acquired during my long training to take over. I feinted toward him and, as he swung a still casual arm in my direction, slipped inside and belted him hard over the heart. Now it was his turn to go sprawling, and there was a roar from the men crowding around us. He got up slowly, his face angry. The others moved back, forming a ring, clearing the tables to do so. I realized I had to go through with it. I was not afraid of that, but I could appreciate my own folly. I had been warned about my rashness by Julius and now, within a week of starting out on an enterprise of such desperate importance, it had already betrayed me.

He rushed at me, and I had to concern myself again with what was present and immediate. I sidestepped and hit him as he went past. Although he was bigger than I was, he was lacking in any kind of skill. I could have danced around him for as long as I liked, cutting him to pieces. But that would not do at all. What was needed was one disabling blow. From every point of view, the sooner this was over the better.

So the next time he attacked I rode his punch with my left shoulder, sank my right fist into the vulnerable area just under his ribs and, stepping back, caught him with as powerful a left hook as I could manage as, gulping air, his head involuntarily came forward. I got a lot of strength into it. He went backward even faster and hit the floor. The watching men were silent. I looked at my fallen opponent and, seeing that he showed no signs of getting up, moved in the direction of the door, expecting that the ring would open to let me through.

But that did not happen. They stared at me sullenly without budging. One of them knelt beside the prone figure.

He said, "He hit his head. He may be hurt badly."

Someone else said, "You ought to get the police."

A few hours later I stared up at the stars, bright in a clear black sky. I was cold and hungry, miserable and self-disgusted. I was a prisoner in the Pit.

I had met very rough justice at the hands of the magistrate who had examined me. The fellow I had knocked out was a nephew of his, a son of a leading merchant in the town. The evidence was that I had provoked him in the tavern by saying things derogatory of the Württembergers, and that I had then hit him when he was not looking. It bore no resemblance at all to what had happened, but there were a number of witnesses who agreed on the story. My opponent was not one of these: he had suffered a concussion when his head hit the floor and he was in no state to say anything to anybody. I was warned that if he failed to recover I would assuredly be hanged. Meanwhile I was to be consigned to the Pit, during the magistrate's pleasure.

This was their preferred way of dealing with malefactors. The Pit was round, some fifteen feet across and about as many feet deep. The floor was of rough flagstones, and the walls were also lined with stones. They were smooth enough to frustrate attempts at climbing up, and there were iron spikes near the top, projecting inward, which further discouraged thoughts of escape. I had been dropped over these like a sack of potatoes, and left. I had been given no food, and had nothing to cover me in a night which looked as though it were going to be cold. I had banged my elbow and grazed my arm in the fall.

But the real fun, as I had been told with satisfaction by some of my captors, would take place the following day. The Pit was designed partly for punishment, partly for the amusement of the local people. It was their custom to stand at the top and pelt the unfortunate prisoner with whatever came to hand or mind. Filth of all kinds—rotting vegetables, slops, that sort of thing—were what they chiefly preferred, but if they were really annoyed they might use stones, billets of wood, broken bottles. In the past prisoners had been severely injured, some even killed. My captors appeared to get a lot of pleasure out of the prospect, and out of telling me about it.

I supposed it was something that the skies had cleared. There was no protection here from the elements. There was, by the wall, a trough with water in it, but although I was thirsty I was not yet thirsty enough to drink from it; there had been enough light, when I was first thrown down, to see that it was covered by a greenish scum. No food was provided to those in the Pit. When they got sufficiently hungry they would eat the rotting refuse, bones and stale bread that were hurled at them. That, too, was supposed to be amusing.

What a fool I had been. I shivered, and cursed my idiocy, and shivered again.

Gradually the night wore through. A couple of times I lay down, curled myself up, and tried to sleep. But it was growing colder, and I had to get up again and walk about to restore my circulation. I longed for the day and dreaded it at the same time. I wondered what had happened to the others—whether Ulf had got back yet. I knew there was no hope of him intervening on my behalf. He was quite well-known in this town, but he dared not take the risk of associating with me. Tomorrow they would go on downriver, leaving me here: there was nothing else they could do.

The wide circle of sky above me brightened—I could tell which side faced east by the softer light there. For a change, I sat with my back to the stone wall. Tiredness, despite the cold, crept over me. My head nodded down to my chest. Then a sound overhead jerked me into wakefulness. There was a face there, peering down. It was a small silhouette against the paling dawn. An early riser, I thought drearily, impatient to get at the victim. It would not be long before the throwing started.

Then a voice, quietly calling down.

"Will—are you all right?"

Beanpole's voice.

He had brought a length of rope from the barge. He stretched down and tied it to one of the iron spikes, then tossed the other end to me. I grabbed it, and hauled myself up. The spikes took some negotiating, but Beanpole was able to get a hand over them to help me. In a matter of seconds I was heaving myself up and being hauled over the edge of the Pit.

We wasted no time in discussing our situation.

The Pit was on the outskirts of the town, which, sleeping still but outlined now in the clear light of dawn, stood between us and the place where the *Erlkönig* was moored. I had only a hazy recollection of being brought here the previous evening, but Beanpole ran confidently and I followed him. It took us perhaps ten minutes to come within sight of the river, and we had seen only one man, in the distance, who shouted something but did not attempt to follow our fleeing figures. Beanpole, I realized, had timed things perfectly. We passed the street where the market had been. In another fifty yards we should be on the quay.

We reached it, and turned left. About as far again along, just past the tavern, next to the barge called *Siegfried.* I stared, and stopped, and Beanpole did the same. The *Siegfried* was there, all right, but next to her the berth was empty.

Beanpole, after a moment, plucked my sleeve. I looked where he indicated, in the opposite direction—to the north. The *Erlkönig* was out in midstream, beating downriver, a quarter of a mile off, a toy boat rapidly diminishing with distance.

Three

A Raft on the River

Our first concern was to get away before my escape from the Pit became known. We went north along the waterfront, through a few mean streets with ramshackle buildings quite unlike the painted and carved and well-cared-for houses in the center of the town, and found a road—little better than a track—which followed the general line of the river. The sun rose on our right, behind the wooded hills. There was cloud there, too, forming with ominous speed. In half an hour it had darkened the sky and blanked out the sun; in three quarters, a gray belt of rain was sweeping down the slope toward us. Five minutes later, already soaking wet, we found some sort of shelter in a ruined building lying back from the road. We had time then to think over what had happened, and what we should do about it.

On the way, Beanpole had told me his side of events. He had not found Ulf, but when he returned to the barge Ulf was there. He *had* been drinking, and it had not improved his temper. He was furious with Beanpole and me for having gone into the town, and with Moritz for having allowed us. We two, he had decided, would spend the remainder of the trip downriver below decks. Fritz, obviously, was the only one who could be relied on, the only one with any sense.

As time passed without my return, his anger increased. After dark, one of the men he knew, calling in to see him, spoke of the young Tiroler who had started a fracas in a tavern, and who in consequence had been condemned to the Pit. When this man had gone, Ulf spoke in an even more angry and implacable fashion. My folly had jeopardized everything. I was clearly a liability to the enterprise rather than an asset. There was to be no more waiting, and certainly no attempt to set me free. In the morning the *Erlkönig* would resume its voyage. It would take two participants to the Games instead of three. As far as I was concerned, I had got myself into the Pit and I could stay there and rot.

Although he did not talk about it, I knew that Beanpole found himself cruelly in a quandary over this. We were under Ulf's authority, and ought to obey him in all things. Moreover, what he said was entirely reasonable. Above all, it was the project itself that mattered, not individuals. His job was to do his best to win at the Games, to gain entry into the City of the Tripods, and to bring out of it information that might help to destroy them. That was what was really important.

But he had talked to Moritz, asking him questions particularly about the Pit—what it was like, where it was situated. I do not know whether Moritz was too stupid to see where the questions might be tending, or whether he saw and approved—he was, I thought, really too amiable a man for work, which, of its nature, required a streak of ruthlessness. Anyway, Beanpole found out what he wanted to know and, at first light, took a length of rope and left the *Erlkönig* in search of me. Presumably Ulf heard or saw something of his departure and either in rage or out of cold logic decided there was nothing for it but to salvage the one reliable member of the trio and get the *Erlkönig* under way before there could be any question of suspicion falling on the boat or its crew.

So here we were, stranded, hundreds of miles short of our objective.

• • •

The rain stopped as abruptly as it had started, and gave way to hot sunlight in which our wet clothes steamed as we walked. We were drenched again less than an hour later—this time there was no shelter at all and the torrential downpour soaked us to our skins—and the day proved to be one of sunburst and cloudburst. Most of the time we were sodden and miserable; all the time we were conscious of the mess we— I in particular—had made of things.

We were also hungry. I had eaten nothing since the previous midday and as soon as the immediate excitement of escape and flight had died down, I was aware of ravenous hunger. We had what was left of the money we had got from Moritz, but there was nowhere, of course, to spend it out in the open country, and we had not fancied waiting in the town until the shops opened. The land through which we were traveling was either waste or pasture, with groups of black-and-white cows chewing their cuds. I proposed milking one, and with Beanpole's assistance cornered her in an angle of a field. But it was a fiasco. I got out no more than a few drops, and she objected strongly to my rough and inexperienced handling and forced her way clear. It did not seem worthwhile trying again.

Several hours after we started, we came on a turnip field. There was a cottage within sight of it, but we risked taking some of the vegetables.

They were unappetizing, but provided something to chew on. The rain came down again as we continued and this time lasted without ceasing for an hour or more.

We found a patch of ruins in which to spend the night. We had discovered no other source of food, and chewed grass and the green shoots of the hedgerow in an attempt to stay our hunger. It was ineffective, and gave us stomach pains. Also, of course, our clothes were wet. We tried to sleep but with poor success. We were awake as night grayed into morning, and set off, tired and wretched, on our way.

It did not actually rain, but the day was cloudy and chilling. The river rolled beside us, broad here and turbulent, and we watched a barge go downstream and thought we detected, in its wake, the fragrance of bacon frying on the galley stove. Not far on, we found a cluster of houses, a farming hamlet, and Beanpole had the idea of presenting himself as a Vagrant, and hoping to be given food. I offered to do it instead, but he said it was his idea, and I must keep out of sight. Vagrants never traveled in company. So I hid in a hedge, and watched.

In my village at home there had been the Vagrant House, provided for the use of these poor wandering madmen: there they were given food and drink, and there were servants to clean and cook. Beanpole had told me that in his country nothing of this sort was provided. Vagrants slept rough and where they could—in barns if they were lucky, or in ruins. They begged their food from door to door, and it was given them with widely varying generosity.

We had assumed that something of the sort might apply here. There were half a dozen houses, and I saw Beanpole go up to the first of them and knock at the door. It did not open; later he told me that a voice from inside had shouted at him to go away, adding curses. At the second door there was no response at all. At the third, a window opened and a bucket of dirty water was thrown over him, to the accompaniment of laughter. As he went away, wetter than before, the door opened. He half turned, prepared to put up with insults if there was a chance of food—and then fled. They had loosed a savage-looking brindle dog on him. It chased him halfway to where I was lying and then stood barking its hostility after him.

Half a mile farther on we found and raided a potato field. They were small, and would have been more palatable cooked. But we had no prospect of making a fire in this cold gray sullen land. We slogged on and, as darkness fell, saw, ahead of us downriver, a barge moored by the bank. I think the same thought struck us both— that it might be the *Erlkönig*, that for some reason Ulf might have been held up and that we might rejoin them. It was an absurd hope, but it was bitter, all the same, to have it dashed. The barge was bigger than the *Erlkönig* and was pointing upstream not down. We moved away from the river to get past it.

Later we came back to the river bank, to sit shivering in a broken-down hut. An unhappy silence had fallen. I wondered if Beanpole were thinking that he might, but for me, have been safe and warm and well fed on the barge. I thought about that myself, though it did no good. Then he said, "Will."

"Yes."

"Where the barge was moored, there was a wharf, and a couple of houses. That would be one of the stages."

"I suppose so."

"The first we have passed since the town."

I thought about that. "Yes, it is."

"Ulf was reckoning to cover two stages a day, taking things easily. So in two days . . ."

In two days we had covered a distance the barge would have sailed in a morning, though we had walked from first light till it was too dark to see where we were going. It was reasonable enough, but discouraging. I made no comment. Beanpole went on, "It was planned that we should get there three days before the opening of the Games. It was to take five days. At this rate, we shall take twenty. The Games will be over before we arrive."

"Yes." I tried to rouse myself from torpor. "Do you think we ought to go back instead?"

"To the Tunnel? I don't like to think what we should say to Julius in that case."

Nor did I, but I did not see what else we could do.

Beanpole said, "We must get on faster. There is the river."

"We dare not approach one of the other barges. You know what was said about that. They're suspicious of strangers and never allow them on board."

"If we had a boat of our own . . ."

"It would be a fine thing," I said, with a touch, I fear, of sarcasm. "Or if we found a Shmand-Fair traveling along the river bank and could climb aboard it."

Beanpole said patiently: "A boat—or a raft? The side of this hut, maybe? It is falling apart, as it is. If we could detach it, and get it into the water . . . the current would carry us at least twice as fast as we could walk, and much more directly."

I took his point, and felt a lift of hope which for a moment allowed me to forget my cold shivering limbs and groaning empty stomach. It just might be possible. Long ago as a boy I had helped to make a raft under the supervision of my cousin Jack, and we had floated it on a nearby duck pond. It had collapsed and precipitated us into pea-soup water and stinking mud. But we had been children then. Yes, it might work.

I said, "Do you think we can . . . ?"

"In the morning," Beanpole said. "We will try in the morning."

The day, as though to encourage us, started bright. We tackled the job at first light. It was encouragingly easy, and then discouragingly difficult. The wall Beanpole had spoken of was about six feet square, and already largely split away from the roof. We completed the separation, and freed the sides. After that it was simple enough to push it outward and down. It collapsed with a satisfying clatter—and in a heap of individual planks.

The thing to do, Beanpole said, was to secure them with cross-pieces. Planks taken from the other walls would do. As for the means of securing them, we would have to take nails out and drive them in again where needed. He spoke with a fine, practical-sounding confidence.

The trouble was that most of the existing nails were both twisted and rusted, in some cases to the point where they broke under simple finger pressure. We had to hunt for reasonably sound ones, to lever them out carefully, avoiding any further distortion, and then to straighten them and drive them through the crossed planks. We had nothing like a hammer, of course. We had to use chunks of stone with fairly flat surfaces. Beanpole found quite a good one and surrendered it to me because, as he said, I could use it better. This was true. I have always been fairly skilled with my hands—more, I am afraid, than with my head.

It was hard work, and took time. We were sweating when we finished, and the sun stood clear above the hills. That left us with the task of getting our raft into the water, and this was not easy, either. The hut was some fifty feet from the river bank, and the ground between was uneven and marshy. The raft was much too heavy to lift; we had to drag and pull and maneuver it, a little at a time, and resting between efforts. Once, when it got entangled in some viciously prickly thorn bushes, I almost felt like giving up, and kicked the planks in angry despair. It was Beanpole who tugged it free. Not long after that, we got it to the bank, and only had to force it down a short slope to the dark rushing waters of the great river. And it was here that, again through Beanpole, we had a stroke of luck: he found the rough nest of a water bird, with four large speckled eggs in it. We ate them raw, licking the inside of the shell with our tongues, and threw ourselves into the final struggle. Beanpole plunged into the river and dragged; I thrust from the other side. The raft creaked ominously, and I saw a nail spring, but she went in and floated. We clambered aboard, and pushed off from the bank.

It was not exactly a triumphant voyage. A current took us out and propelled us, spinning round in sluggish circles, downstream. She floated, but only just. Under our combined weights, all but one corner was under water. Through some freak of balance this rode some inches above the level of the river: we took it in turns, for one of us to crouch there while the other sat or sprawled in the slopping wet. The water was cold, too, as well it might be at this time of the year, in a river whose early course was fed by the melting snows of the southern mountains.

But at least we were getting on faster than we had done by land. The bank flowed past us at a steady rate. And the weather was holding fine. The sun blazed hot in a sky whose blue was reflected, more deeply, in the smooth thoroughfare along which we traveled. Beanpole called to me, and pointed. To the west there was a Tripod, giant-striding through the fields. I felt a kind of satisfaction at the sight. Ridiculously puny by comparison though we were, it was something that we were still in the fight.

The next time I saw a Tripod I was a good deal less happy about it.

An hour after we set out, we passed a barge. It was heading upstream, and the encounter was therefore a brief one. A man on deck stared at us curiously, and threw out some comment or question which we did not grasp. We must have presented an odd sight, floating along on this waterlogged contraption.

Hunger had been scarcely abated by the four raw eggs, and became more and more insistent. We saw fields which looked as though they held crops which might be worth raiding, but here a particular deficiency of our ramshackle craft was brought home to us—our inability to steer it. We had a couple of plank splinters, but they were only of value in pushing the raft away from obstacles, and not much then. I realized that we must go where the river took us, and that, apart from the chance of running aground, we could only make a landfall by abandoning the raft and swimming for it. We were well out now, and the current was strong; it would have taken quite a swim to make the shore. Meanwhile, the fields slid by and gave way, after a time, to terraces planted with the regular ranks of vines. But even if we could get at them, the grapes would be tiny at this season.

A large fish, possibly a salmon, leaped tantalizingly near us. We had no means of cooking it, but if we had been able to catch it we would have had a shot at eating it raw. Visions of food passed before me, as I clung to the sodden wood. Beef roasting on a spit . . . tender leg of lamb, with the sauce my mother made from garden mint . . . or just bread and cheese—bread crusty outside and soft within, cheese yellow and crumbling to the touch. I tasted my own spit, salt and unsatisfying.

The hours passed. The sun arched high behind us and then curved down to the west. I was both hot and cold. I tried drinking great quantities of water, scooping it up in my hands, to fill the aching void in my belly, but it only made me feel bloated without being any less hungry. In the end, I told Beanpole that we must get food somehow. We had passed two villages, one on either bank of the river. There would be food there, something edible at least—in the gardens if we could not manage anything better. If we worked hard to paddle ourselves in toward shore with the bits of wood we had . . . and then did our best to beach the raft at the next sign of human habitation . . .

He said, "It would be better if we could hold out till evening. There will be more opportunity to forage."

"We may not see a village then."

We argued, and at last, reluctantly, he agreed. We had moved, by degrees, nearer the west bank, and we tried paddling toward that. The result was ludicrous. The raft spun around but our position relative to the shore did not alter. We abandoned the attempt, realizing we were getting nowhere.

Beanpole said, "It's no good."

I said, "Then we'll have to swim for it."

"That means abandoning the raft."

Of course it did. I was angry. "We can't go on without food! It was a mad idea to try this, anyway, without any means of controlling it."

Beanpole was silent. Still irritated, I said, "And what about tonight? We can't sleep here. If we tried to we would roll off and drown. We shall have to abandon it before dark, anyway."

"Yes," he said, "I agree. But let us wait longer. There are no houses now."

That was true. The river rolled between green banks devoid of any signs of life. I said sullenly, "I suppose so. Isn't it time we changed over again?"

Later there was a deserted jumble of ruins, and north of that we met another barge. There was a temptation to shout to them to pick us up. I resisted it, with difficulty. We had passed a staging post soon after noon—it had been empty, the small wharf white and silent in the harsh sunlight. The second post had two barges tied up and a mile farther on a third barge was nosing its way south. I had not said anything else about leaving the raft and swimming for shore: Beanpole knew as well as I that this was what we would have to do. I took a perverse satisfaction in leaving it to him now to initiate things.

And as the day waned we saw ruins again,

but still no sign of habitation. The river was wider, and we had drifted out into the center. The swim would not be easy under any circumstances, still less to two people who were hungry and exhausted, cold and wet. The resentment I had felt against Beanpole faded in the prospect of what lay ahead.

Quite suddenly, though, everything changed. It came from the north, striding along the west bank. It was going to pass no more than a hundred yards from us, closer than any Tripod had been on this trip. There was no satisfaction now; only a great relief when it had gone past.

Until I saw it swing around and turn toward us, and heard the ululation which I had twice heard before and had good cause to dread. Water fountained up as the great metal feet splashed into the river. We had become a target; there could be no doubt of that. I stared at Beanpole, and he stared back. I said, "Better dive for it."

It was already too late. At that instant the metal tentacle snaked down from the hemisphere. It crashed between us, splintering the frail planks. The next moment we were struggling in the water.

Four

The Hermit of the Island

I had been expecting to be snatched up by a tentacle. The Tripod's action, of smashing the raft instead, astonished as well as frightened me. I went deep under and took a mouthful of river water before I fully realized what was happening. When I surfaced, I looked up and saw that the Tripod, silent again, was rocking away on its previous course to the south. It seemed that what it had done had been aimless, on a par with the waltzing around the *Orion* when we were crossing the Channel from England. Like a vicious boy it had noticed something strange, swatted it out of pointless malice, and gone its way.

But survival was a more pressing concern than speculation on the motives of the Tripods. The raft had disintegrated into its component planks, one of which bobbed on the water near me. A couple of strokes took me to it, and I hung on and looked for Beanpole. I could see nothing but the river, graying with the approach of evening, and wondered if the tip of the tentacle might have struck him as it came down. Then I heard his voice and, turning my head to look back, saw him swimming in my direction. He took the other end of the plank and we trod water, gasping.

I said, "Shall we strike out for the shore?"

He had a fit of coughing; then said:

"Not yet, I think. Look ahead. The river bends. If we hang on we may be taken nearer in."

The plank in any case was a support which I was not eager to relinquish. The current seemed faster, and certainly more turbulent. There were hills on either side, the river forcing itself between them. We were coming to the angle where it turned, fairly sharply, to the west. As we did so, I saw the green bank on our right divide, and had a glimpse of more water.

"The river . . ." I said. "It must fork there."

"Yes," Beanpole said. "Will, I think we must swim for it now."

I had learned to swim in the rivers around

my village of Wherton, and once or twice, illic-
itly, in the lake up at the estate. Beanpole,
though, had grown up in a seaside town. He
pulled away from me with powerful strokes,
realized I was falling behind, and called out,
"Are you all right?"

I called back doggedly, "All right," and concentrated on swimming. The current was very
strong. The shore at which I was aiming slid
quickly past. Then I saw something which dis-
mayed me. Ahead the shore became a spit, with
beyond it a wider reach of water. It was not a
true fork in the river, but an island. If I missed
landing on it there was the wider passage before
me. Already tired, I would find myself in midstream with a much longer haul ahead. I altered
course, and swam almost directly against the current. I heard Beanpole call again, but could not
spare the energy to look for him or to reply. I
struggled on, my arms becoming more and more
leaden, the water colder and fiercer and more
implacable. I no longer looked where I was
heading, concerned only with forcing my arms
through the water. Then something hit my head
and I went under, dazed. I remembered nothing
after that until I was aware of someone dragging
me, and of firm ground under my feet.

It was Beanpole who pulled me up on to a
grassy bank. When I had recovered enough to
take in my surroundings, I saw by how small a

margin we had made it. We were within a few yards of the northernmost limit of the island. It lay in the center of the river's bend, and just ahead the river did broaden considerably. I discovered my head was hurting, and put my hand up to my forehead.

"A plank hit you," Beanpole said. "From the raft, I think. How do you feel, Will?"

"A bit dizzy," I said. Something else returned. "And hungry. Across there—isn't it . . . ?"

"Yes," he said, "a village."

Despite the deepening dusk, it was possible to see houses on the east bank; some had lights in their windows. By this time I would have been prepared to take a chance on having dirty water thrown over me or being chased by large dogs— even on being questioned as to what I was doing here. But not on trusting myself to the river again; I could think more clearly but physically I was as weak as though I had spent a month in bed.

"We will get across in the morning," Beanpole said.

"Yes." I nodded wearily. "In the morning."

"The trees are thicker farther back. More shelter, if it rains."

I nodded again, and moved my leaden legs forward. For a few steps only, and then stopped. Someone was standing by the edge of the trees, watching us. When he realized we had seen him, he came toward us. In the dim light I could see that he was a man in his middle years, tall and lean, dressed in rough-looking dark trousers and shirt, his hair long and his face bearded. I saw something else, too. Although his hair hung down behind his neck, it receded at the forehead. It was dark hair, beginning to turn gray. And where the silver band of the Cap should have been there was only flesh, toughened and browned by long years of exposure.

He spoke in German, in a harsh dialect. He had been looking out and had seen us struggling in the water, had watched Beanpole haul me in to shore. His manner was odd, I thought—part grudging and part welcoming. I had the feeling that he would have been quite happy to see us drift on past, and would not have spared more than a moment's thought for our chances of escaping drowning. But now that we were here . . .

He said, "You'll want to dry yourselves out. You'd better come with me."

All sorts of questions were in my mind, apart from the really crucial one of why he was not Capped. But it seemed best to do as he said, and let enlightenment wait. I looked at Beanpole and he nodded. The man led the way, up to what I saw was a well-trodden path. It wound between the trees for several minutes before coming out into a clearing. In front of us there was a wooden hut, with an oil lamp burning in the window, smoke blowing from its chimney. He unlatched the door and went inside, we following.

A log fire was burning in a stone fireplace. There was a large woolen rug in front of it—red with a design of black and yellow animals—and sitting on the rug there were three cats. Two of them were tabbies, marked with white patches, the third an oddly patterned black-and-white with a white face and a funny black moustache under the nose. The man moved them with his foot, not roughly, merely forcing them to yield place. He went to a cupboard, and produced two lengths of coarse toweling.

"Get your wet things off," he said. "Warm yourselves in front of the fire. I've got a couple of shirts and trousers you can put on while your own are drying." He stared at us. "Are you hungry?"

We looked at each other. Beanpole said, "Very hungry, sir. If you . . ."

"Don't call me sir. I'm Hans. Bread and cold ham. I don't usually cook at night."

"Just bread will do," I said.

"Aye," he said. "You look starved. Get yourselves dry, then."

The trousers and shirt were too big, of course, particularly in my case. I had to roll the bottoms up and he gave me a belt to put around the middle. I was lost inside the shirt. While we were changing, he had been putting things on a scrubbed wooden table under the window: a couple of knives, plates, a dish of yellow butter, a large flat loaf of brown bread and a ham, partly cut, which showed firm pink meat surrounded by clear white fat, baked brown on the outside. I sliced at it, while Beanpole cut bread. I saw Hans watching me, and was a little ashamed of the thickness of the slices I was cutting. But he nodded, approvingly. He brought over a couple of mugs, plonked them by our plates, and returned with a big earthenware jar from which he poured us dark drafts of beer. We set to. I warned myself to eat slowly, but it was no good. The ham was sweet and good, the bread nutty and coarse textured, the butter of a finer quality than I had tasted since leaving home. The beer with which I washed it down was strong and sweet. My jaws ached with chewing, but my belly still clamored for nourishment.

Hans said, "You were hungry, all right." I looked guiltily at my plate. "Never mind. Eat on. I like to see someone enjoying his victuals."

I came to a halt at last—Beanpole had finished much earlier. I was feeling full, in fact overfull, and happy. The room was snug, with the glow of lamplight and the flicker of firelight and the three cats, back in their original positions, purring away in the hearth. I presumed that now we would be asked questions—where we had come from, the reason for our being in the river. But this did not happen. Our host sat in a wooden rocking chair which looked as though he might have made it himself, and smoked a pipe. He did not seem to find the silence awkward or constraining. In the end, it was Beanpole who said:

"Could you tell us how it is that you are not Capped?"

Hans took his pipe from his mouth. "I've never bothered."

"Not bothered!"

It came out slowly, through prodding from both of us. His father had brought him to this island as a young boy, after his mother died. The pair of them had lived together here, growing their own vegetables, keeping chickens and a few pigs, making things to sell in the village across the river. Then his father had died, in turn, and he had stayed on. No one from the village troubled about him; he was not counted as part of their life. This had happened in the spring of the year in which he would have been Capped, and during that summer he had not moved from the island, concerned with doing on his own all the things in which previously he had assisted his father. (He had buried his father, he told us, not far from the hut, and over slow months next winter carved a stone with his name to put over his grave.) Since then he had gone across to the village perhaps twice a year. He had a boat in which he rowed there and back.

At first I was incredulous, thinking of the trouble all we who had fled to the White Mountains had taken to avoid being Capped, while this man had just stayed where he was, not worrying. Surely there could not be flaws like this in the Tripods' mastery of the earth? But the more I thought about it, the less surprising it seemed. He was one man, living like a hermit. The domination of the Tripods depended on the serfdom of men as such, and to that end it was enough that Capping should be accepted as a natural and inevitable thing where a handful of men, two or three even, were gathered together. One man did not matter, as long as he stayed quiet and caused no trouble. And the moment he did cause trouble, of course, he would be dealt with, either by the Tripods or their human servants.

Beanpole, once he had established all this, quizzed him about the Tripods. Did he see much of them? What did he feel about them? I saw where the line of questioning was heading, and was content to leave it to him. He did not seem surprised at or suspicious of the conversation, and this in itself showed how small his contact with the wider world must have been. Local customs varied in different countries, but in every one the subject of Tripods and Caps was covered by a taboo. No one, Capped as we appeared to be, would have spoken like this.

But if unsuspicious, he was also indifferent. He saw the Tripods from time to time, yes. He believed they damaged crops on the mainland; it was hard to see how they could avoid it, great massive things like they were. But none of them, he was glad to say, had ever planted its heavy foot on this island. As for Caps, well, people wore them, and they didn't seem to do a lot of harm and didn't seem to do any particular good. He believed it was something to do with the Tripods, since the boys who went for Capping were taken up by the Tripods. Did they prevent people wanting to fight against the Tripods? Beanpole asked daringly.

Hans looked at him over his pipe. He said shrewdly:

"Well, you'd know more about that than I do, would you not? But it wouldn't make a lot of sense wanting to fight against the Tripods, would it? You would have to be pretty strong in the arm to throw a stone high enough to hit that part at the top, and what good would it do you if you did? For that matter, what's the point in it? It's not as though they do much harm. A bit of damage now and then to crops and cattle—to men, maybe, if they don't get out of the way fast enough. But lightning can kill you with less chance of dodging, and hailstones can ruin crops."

Beanpole said, "We were on a raft farther up the river. The raft was smashed by a Tripod. That's how we came to be washed up here."

Hans nodded. "Bad luck comes to everyone. Some sickness got among my hens two years back. Wiped out all but three of them."

"We're very grateful to you," Beanpole said, "for giving us food and shelter."

Hans stared from his face to the fire, and back.

"As to that, I get along without seeing people well enough, but now you're here . . . There's some wood that needs cutting, up at the top end. I've had rheumatics in my shoulder, and it's not got done. You can get on with that tomorrow, and it will pay for the food you eat, and your lodging. Later, maybe, I'll row you across to the village."

Beanpole started to say something; then stopped and merely nodded. There was silence again, Hans staring into the fire. I said, "But if you found people who were fighting against the Tripods—wouldn't you help them? After all, you are a free man."

He looked at me for some moments before replying.

"That's strange talk," he said. "I don't have a

lot to do with people, but it sounds strange talk to me. You don't come from these parts, lad."

It was part accusation, part question. I said, "But if there *were* men who were not slaves of the Tripods. Surely you would want to do what you could . . ."

I found my voice trailing off under the steady regard of the bearded man.

"Strange talk," he repeated. "I mind my own business. I always have, and I always will. Are you one of those they call Vagrants, maybe? But they travel around by themselves, not in couples. I don't have trouble with anyone, because I keep out of it. You seem to want to start trouble. If that's the way you think . . ."

Beanpole cut in on him. He said, with a quick look of warning at me, "You mustn't pay any attention to him, Hans. He's feeling queer. When he was in the water, he was hit on the head by one of the planks from the raft. You can see the bruise on his forehead."

Hans got up from his feet, and came toward me. He peered at my head for a long time. Then he said, "Aye. He's maybe addled his wits a bit. It won't hinder him from swinging an axe in the morning. But you'll both benefit from a good night's sleep. I rise early, so I don't stay up late."

He brought blankets from the hut's other room, in which he slept. Then with a gruff good-night he left us, taking the lamp with him.

Beanpole and I settled ourselves down on the floor, on either side of the fire. I was feeling vaguely uncomfortable from the supper which, following the previous days' privation, was not proving easy to digest. I expected to have a restless night. But tiredness was stronger than queasiness.

I looked at the glow of the fire, the three cats still sentinel in front of it; and my next sight was of sunlight on cold ashes, the cats gone, and Hans, whose heavy tread had wakened me, calling to us to get up.

The breakfast he prepared for us was enormous. Great slices of grilled gammon with as many eggs as we wanted (I ate three), and hot, golden-brown potato cakes. With it we drank more of the beer he had given us the previous night.

"Eat well," Hans said. "The more you eat, the better you'll work."

He took us with him to the north of the island. There was a field of about an acre, under potatoes, and he explained that he wanted to extend it by cutting down and rooting out the trees in the adjoining copse. He had started this task, but the rheumatism in his shoulder had first hindered and then entirely prevented him. He provided us with axe, spade, and mattock, watched us while we set to, and left us.

It was hard work. The standing trees were green and supple, and the roots of those already cut down were tangled and hard to dig out. Beanpole suggested that if we worked hard he might regard a morning's work as sufficient return for hospitality and take us across the river in the afternoon. But although we sweated at the job, the going proved slow. When Hans came for us, toward midday, he looked critically at our results.

"I thought you would have done better than that. Still, you've made a start. You'd better come now for your dinner."

He had roasted a couple of chickens, and he served these with a heap of buttered potatoes and a sour-tasting cabbage. He gave us wine with it, because beer, he said, was likely, in the middle of the day, to make us sluggish. Afterward there were sweet blueberries, doused with cream. Then he said, "You can rest now for half an hour, and digest your food, while I get things cleared up. Then you get back to the field. Leave that big oak till tomorrow. I want to make sure she falls the right way."

He left us lying in the sun. I said to Beanpole, "Tomorrow? So much for him offering to take us across the river this afternoon."

Beanpole said slowly, "Tomorrow, and the day after, and the day after that. He is determined to keep us here until the wood is cleared."

"But that would take a week, at least, probably two!"

Beanpole said, "Yes. And we're already behind time for competing in the Games."

"We shall not manage that, anyway, on foot. We should have to find the material for another raft, and build it. And even then I doubt if we could do it. We need a boat."

I stopped as the idea struck home, surprised that it had not occurred to me before. We had seen Hans's boat on our way up to the field. It was tied in a small inlet on the east of the island, a sturdy-looking six-footer, with a pair of oars. Beanpole, from the look he gave me, was thinking along the same lines.

I said, "If we managed to slip away this evening . . . I suppose it would be a rotten trick, but . . ."

"The boat must mean a great deal to him," Beanpole said. "He depends on it to get to and from the village. I think probably he built it himself, or his father did, and it would take him a long time to build another, particularly with the pains in his shoulder. But we know from what he said last night that he would never help us, although he is not Capped. He would keep us here, working for him, even if he knew what our mission was. I think getting into the City is more important, Will, than this lonely old man and his boat."

"So, this evening . . ."

"This evening loses us half a day, and there may not be another time when we know ourselves to be unwatched." He rose to his feet. "I think now is better."

We walked in as innocent a manner as possible toward the shelter of the trees. As we approached them, I glanced back and saw the open door of the hut, but no sign of Hans. We went more quickly after that, running in the direction of the inlet and the boat. It rocked as Beanpole climbed aboard and unshipped the oars, while I saw to the rope that secured it to the branch of a tree. It was tied in a complicated knot, over which I struggled with, at first, little effect.

Beanpole said, "Hurry, Will."

"If I had a knife . . ."

"I think I hear someone."

I heard, too—running feet and now a voice, calling harshly. I wrenched desperately at the knot, and it came free. Then I scrambled into the boat, which tilted dangerously under us. As Beanpole pushed off from the bank, the figure of Hans burst through from the trees, shouting curses. We were ten feet clear by the time he reached the water's edge. He did not stop but plunged in after us. The fast-flowing water came up to his knees, his thighs, but he waded on, still cursing. When it reached his waist, he even succeeded in grasping at the blade of one of the oars, but Beanpole pulled it from him. The current took us, and we moved out toward midstream.

He fell silent then, and his expression changed. I had borne his earlier raving and anger easily enough, but this was different. I can still feel sick when I remember the terrible despair in his face.

We went downriver swiftly enough after that. We took it in turns at the oars, started early and carried on until late each day. Food was a problem, but we managed, although we were, after the first day, hungry all the time. We passed barges, traveling upstream and down, and kept clear of them—a course increasingly easy as the great river broadened on its way to the sea. The river itself was a source of much interest, rolling through varied scenery, woods, pastures, vineyards, and wheat fields and the silent somber heaps, mounded up on either side, of the ruined cities of the ancients. We saw Tripods many times, and once heard the wild warbling of their hunting call, but that was far in the distance. None approached us closely. There were rivers that ran in to join the mother river, castles of great antiquity lifted high on spurs of cliff, and in one place a huge tawny mass of tree-decked rock, taller than a Tripod, set in midstream.

And so finally we came to where the Games were held. There were many barges tied up there, the *Erlkönig* among them.

Five

The Games

It was a land of flower-starred meadows, heavy rich-yielding earth, small prosperous villages and everywhere windmills, their sails turning slowly in warm gusts of wind. The season was perhaps not so far advanced as in the south, but the weather seemed to have set in fair. This was true Games weather, people said, though I thought the fact that so many of them remarked on it might indicate that true Games weather was more a rarity than a reasonable expectation.

The town lay west of the river, behind meadows which, as we made our way through them, were hot and slumbrous in the afternoon sun. Many people were traveling that way; not only competitors but spectators to watch the Games. The town and nearby villages seemed to bulge with them, and thousands more set up tents in the fields. There was an air of festival, much eating and drinking of beer and last year's wine—everyone, it seemed, happy, and dressed in their best. We had got there the day before the opening. That night we must sleep where best we could—in the open, as it proved, under willow trees beside a rushing stream—but tomorrow, provided we passed the early trials and were accepted, we would be competitors, to be housed in the long low wooden huts built near the Field.

To reach that place one passed through the town, with its great twin-towered church and its newly painted houses, and skirted the hill that looked down on it. (Wandering there once, we found a vast semicircular pit, descending in levels faced with stone to a central stone platform—we could not guess its purpose, but the stones were cracked and worn and distorted by what must have been not years but centuries. And all those centuries, I thought, before the coming of the Tripods—generation on generation.) Beyond there was a village, and nearby the Field. It was huge in extent, and the local people told a story of it. In the days of the ancients, they said, there had been many great battles, in which—though it was scarcely to be believed—men had slaughtered each other because of their wickedness. This was the field of the last, most immense and savage battle of all, though where some said it had happened, others believed it was still to take place. Hearing this, I hoped it was an omen for our success. One battle needed to be fought, and we, here, were the outriders of our army.

We had seen Moritz at the barge, but not Ulf, who was off drinking. Moritz was pleased to see us, but urged us not to stay because Ulf's anger was still strong, and not likely to be much appeased by our having got here in time after all. Fritz, he told us, had gone up to the Field that morning.

There were flags and banners in all the towns and villages nearby, and they surrounded the Field like the fluttering petals of a thousand huge and gaudy flowers. Behind and above were the tiers of wood on which people sat and watched, with peddlers moving among them selling trinkets and ribbons, sweetmeats, wine, and hot sausages. Projecting from one side was the judges' pavilion, with the dais in front to which the winners would come to claim their champions' belts. To which, we fervently hoped, we ourselves would go.

On the first day, those who were obviously unsuitable were weeded out. We had not felt any doubt that we should qualify, and we did so easily.

I was set to box with a boy of roughly my own age and weight, and in less than a minute the judge put an end to the bout and sent me to be weighed and entered. I met Fritz again in the tent which had been set aside for these procedures. He showed neither surprise at my appearance nor curiosity as to how I had got here. I told him Beanpole was here, too, and he nodded. Three chances were better than one. I had the notion, though, that all along he had believed that it was he who would succeed in getting into the City—that we were not to be relied on.

Later, I found Beanpole again: he, also, had qualified without difficulty, clearing the required distance, in both jumps, by an easy margin. We went together to the dining tent for our midday meal: we were given our food as well as a bed. I asked him how he felt about his chances, now that the challenge was on us. He said seriously, "All right, I think. I did not have to try hard. And you, Will?"

"The one I beat has qualified, too. I saw him in the hut."

"That sounds good. Do you think we ought to look for Fritz?"

"There'll be time, later. Let's eat first."

The next morning there was the opening ceremony. People came in procession from the town, carrying the banners of the Games, and the Games Captain, an old white-haired man who was the leader of the officials, made a speech of welcome to the contestants assembled on the Field, full of phrases about sportsmanship and honor.

I might have been impressed if it were not for those others who were also present. During the tournament at the Chateau de la Tour Rouge, one Tripod had stood above the castle, in silent scrutiny of events. Here there were six. They had marched in early in the morning and were already present, lined up around the Field, when we awoke. Words like sportsmanship and honor had a hollow sound when one remembered that the purpose of these sports was to provide slaves for these metal monsters. Slaves, or sacrifices. After all, though hundreds of men and women each year entered the City, none had yet been known to come out.

There was no boxing on that day, and I was able to watch the preliminaries in the other events. Fritz was entered for the Hundred and Two Hundred Meters races. These were popular lists: for the first there were to be twelve heats, ten entrants in each, with the first and second runners going through to three further races in which the first three qualified. Fritz came second in the fourth heat. This could have been misleading, of course, but it looked to me, watching, as though he were straining hard. The first part of the Long Jump was held in the afternoon, and Beanpole won easily, half a meter ahead of his nearest rival.

My own first trial came the following morning. My opponent was a tall, skinny lad, who moved quickly but was almost entirely defensive. I chased him around the ring, missing occasionally but landing punches more often, and had no doubt about the result. Later in the day I fought again, and again won easily. Beanpole had been watching. Afterward, I put on the track suit which they had given me, and we went to watch the field events. The Two Hundred Meters heats were being run. Beanpole strained his eyes toward the announcement board, but had to ask me which had been reached. I told him Seven.

"Then Fritz has already run," he said. "His heat was Six. Are the results up?"

"They're going up now."

The results board was to one side of the judges' pavilion. It had an elaborate system of trapdoors and ladders and ledges behind it, through which a troupe of boys put up the numbers of the winners. The numbers of the qualifiers in Heat Six appeared on the board while I watched.

Beanpole said, "Well?"

I shook my head. "No."

Beanpole made no comment, nor did I. Fritz's

elimination from one of his two events was our first major setback, forcing us to the realization that there might be others. It would be sickening if we were all forced back, defeated, from this first obstacle; but the possibility had to be reckoned with.

And for me, personally, the possibility became very real the next time I fought. This opponent, like the first, was fast, but he was more skilled and much more aggressive. In the initial round he landed several good punches, and made me miss when I counterattacked, once leaving me tangled with the rope. I had no doubt in my mind that I had lost the round, and was in a fair way to losing the contest. When we came out again I concentrated on getting in close and punching to the body. I did better, but I had a feeling I was still behind on points. I went into the last round in a desperate mood. I attacked in a fury which rattled my opponent. He opened up his guard and I caught him with a right to the side of the head which floored him. He got up at once, but he was nervous after that and tried to keep his distance. He was also plainly tiring, probably from the body blows in the previous round.

I was confident, by the time the final bell went, that I had made up lost ground, but could not be sure how much. I saw the three judges conferring together. They were taking longer than usual about it, and my uncertainty and apprehension curdled into physical sickness. I was trembling when we went back to the center of the ring, and could scarcely believe it when the referee lifted my arm in the sign of victory.

Fritz and Beanpole had both been watching. Beanpole said, "I thought you were going to lose that one."

I was still feeling shaky, but with relief now. I said, "So did I."

"You left it late," Fritz said.

"Not as late as you did in the Two Hundred Meters."

It was a cheap and silly riposte, but Fritz did not rise to it. He said simply, "That is true. So I must concentrate on the other race."

His imperturbability, I supposed, was a good quality, but I found it very irritating.

Two things happened in the afternoon: Fritz qualified for the finals of the Hundred Meters, and Beanpole was eliminated from the High Jump. Fritz again came second, but the winner was yards ahead of him at the tape, and I did not think much of his eventual chances. Beanpole was very depressed by his defeat. Up to the last raising of the bar he had been jumping well and confidently, and seemed certain of going through, but at that point his coordination failed him, and in his first jump he went off at half-cock and ludicrously hit the bar waist-high. His second jump was a good deal better, but still an obvious failure. On the third, I thought he had cleared it but he must have just caught the bar with his foot.

"Bad luck," I said.

His face, as he pulled on the track suit, was white with anger against himself.

"How *could* I jump so badly?" he said. "I've cleared a lot higher than that dozens of times. And now, when it matters . . ."

"There's still the Long Jump."

"I just couldn't get the lift . . ."

"Forget about it. There's no point in brooding."

"It's easy to say that."

"Remember what Fritz said. Concentrate on the other one."

"Yes. I suppose it's good advice."

He did not look convinced.

So we came to the day of the finals. In the evening there would be a procession to the town, where the Feast of the Games was held, with all the competitors honored but the victors in their scarlet belts most of all. And the morning after they would parade on the Field, on show for the last time before the Tripods picked them up to take them to their City.

It had been very hot during the night, and

the sky was no longer blue but livid with cloud, which looked as though it might open at any moment to pour down torrential rain. Thunder rumbled in the distance. If it did rain, the events were to be postponed to the following day. I stared at the sky from the door of the hut, and prayed that it would hold off. I felt I was tensed to the limit already. I tried to force myself to eat some breakfast, but the food would not go down.

Beanpole's event was scheduled first, mine second, and Fritz's third. Concentrating on watching him jump was a torment but at least it took my mind off my own prospects. He jumped well, and it was clear that there were only two others who might match him. They were before him in the order, and on the first jump there was a matter of inches between their marks, with the rest out of the running. On the second jump their results were much the same, but this time Beanpole outdistanced them to take the lead. I saw him walk back from the pit, brushing sand from his leg, and thought: he has it now.

One of the others fell badly short on the final jump. But the second, a gangling freckle-faced boy whose hair sprouted in bright ginger tufts through the silver mesh of the Cap, did much better and his jump put him in the lead. The difference was nine centimeters—about four inches by our English measurement—which was not much in itself but disheartening at this stage. I watched Beanpole tense himself, run down the grassy track, hurl his body through the humid air. A cry went up: it was quite clearly the best jump of the day. But the cry turned to a groan of disappointment as the judge's flag was lifted. The jump had been disqualified, and the ginger-headed boy had won.

Beanpole went off by himself. I followed him, and said, "It couldn't be helped. You did your best."

He looked at me with a blank expression. "I stepped on the board. I haven't done that since the early days of training."

"You were putting too much effort into it. It could happen to anybody."

"Was I?"

"Of course you were."

Beanpole said, "I wanted to win. And also I was frightened about what came next. I thought I was trying."

"We could all see you were."

"In the High Jump," he said, "I went to pieces at the crucial moment. And this time I got myself disqualified quite stupidly and unnecessarily. I thought I was trying, but was I?"

"What you're saying is stupid. You were just trying too hard."

The blankness had turned to misery.

"Leave me alone, Will," he said. "I don't want to talk at the moment."

• • •

The boxing finals were early in the afternoon, and my section provided the second contest. The boy I was fighting was a North German, a fisherman's son, smaller even than I was, but compact and well muscled. I had seen him box and knew that he was good, a fast mover and a hard hitter.

For the first minute we circled each other warily. Then he came in at me with a quick left and right, which I parried, and I counterattacked, forcing him to the ropes and getting in a right cross to the ribs which made him grunt as breath was forced from his lungs. But he got away before I could do any further damage. We fought at a distance again, but in the last thirty seconds I carried the fight to him and scored a few times. It was my round, I thought.

I went out confidently for the second. He backed away, and I followed. He was almost on the ropes. I threw a left hook at his jaw. It did not miss by much, but it missed. And the next thing I remembered was lying on the canvas, with the referee standing over me, counting.

". . . *Drei, vier, fünf* . . ."

It was an uppercut, Beanpole told me later, which did not travel far and caught me under the chin, lifting and dumping me. All I knew then was that I was simultaneously floating in a haze of pain and rooted to the hard boards beneath me. I supposed I ought to get up, but I did not see how I was going to set about it. Nor did there seem much urgency. There appeared to be long intervals between the words that were being chanted, at once close above me and from an echoing distance.

" . . . *Sechs, sieben . . .*"

I had lost, of course, but I had done my best, at any rate. Like Beanpole. I saw his set, bitter face through the haze. "I thought I was trying, but was I?" And what about me? I had been hit because I had dropped my guard. Had something at the back of my mind wanted to do that? Was there even now the beginning of a feeling: you did your best and lost, so no one can blame you? You can go back to the White Mountains, instead of the City of the Tripods. And with it the beginning of a doubt which would not easily be dismissed.

"*Acht!*"

Somehow I got to my feet. I could not see straight, and was staggering. The boy from the North came after me. I managed to dodge some blows and ride others, but I had small idea how. For the remainder of the round he chased me, and once caught me in a corner and gave me a hammering. I did not go down again, but I knew as I sat on my stool and the cool sponge was rubbed over my flesh that I was desperately far behind on points. I would have to knock him out to win.

He realized this, too. After his first probing had established that I was no longer dazed, he did not try to take the fight to me but boxed from a distance. I went after him, but he stood me off. I was gaining a few points, probably, but nothing like the number I had lost. And the seconds were ticking away on the big wooden clock, which stood on the judge's table and was started at the beginning of each round and stopped three minutes later.

In the end, I grew desperate. I abandoned my own defense, deliberately this time, and went on hitting as fast and as often as I could. Most of my blows failed to land, whereas he got in a couple to the body which rocked me. But I kept on, fighting not boxing, forcing in the hope that somehow something would give. And it did. He measured me for a punch that would have finished the job the uppercut had started, and missed. And I did not miss with my own hook to the jaw. His knees buckled and he went down, and I was sure he was not going to get up by a count of ten or, for that matter, fifty. The only doubt I had was whether the bell would go before the count was completed—I had an idea we were in the final seconds. But my mind had been playing me tricks. I learned, to my astonishment, that less than a minute had elapsed of this last round.

• • •

Beanpole and I watched the final of the Hundred Meters in silence, concealing our different feelings. But our silence was shattered when it became apparent that Fritz was keeping up with the runner who had outclassed him in the previous heat. We were both shouting as the two of them crossed the tape. Beanpole thought Fritz had won, I that he had just lost. It was some time before the announcement came, and it proved us both wrong. There had been no clear winner. The race would be rerun, with these two competitors only.

And this time Fritz made no mistake. He went into the lead right away and held it to win comfortably. I cheered with the others, and fervently. I would far rather it had been Beanpole, but I was glad that, at any rate, I would have one ally when I went into the City.

That evening, during the Feast, the heavens opened, thunder rolled almost continuously, and through the high windows I saw lightning playing across the roofs of the town. We ate rich food in enormous quantities, and drank a wine that bubbled in the glass and tingled in one's throat. And I sat at the High Table, wearing my scarlet belt with the rest.

In the morning, as we paraded, a light drizzle was still falling. The Field itself was waterlogged, and our shoes were clogged with mud. I had said good-bye to Beanpole and told him that I hoped I would meet him again, and soon, in the White Mountains.

But the hope was a faint and feeble one. The six Tripods stood, fixed as they had been throughout the Games, while the ceremony of farewell was gone through. I looked at the faces of my companions, all happy and exalted at the thought of serving the Tripods, and did my best to put the same expression on my own. My legs trembled. I made an effort and controlled them, but moments later they were trembling again.

There were more than thirty of us, in six groups. I saw the group with Fritz in it go first, marching toward the Tripod immediately ahead. The tentacle snaked down as they came close to the great metal foot and lifted them, in turn, to the hole that opened in the hemisphere, the hole into which, nearly a year before, I had thrown the exploding metal egg of the ancients. I had no defense now, and could have none. I watched the next group go, and the third and fourth. Then it was our turn and, splashing through puddles, I walked woodenly forward with the rest.

Six

The City of Gold and Lead

What chiefly worried me was that my true feelings would show when the tentacle gripped me—that I would not be able to avoid straining against it and marking myself as different from the others. I even wondered if the tentacle could somehow read my thoughts: I remembered the feel of it—hard metal but weirdly resilient, pulsing with what seemed like life. When it was my turn to be lifted, I did my best to blank out what was happening. I thought instead of my home, of lazy afternoons wandering through the fields, of swimming in the river with my cousin Jack. Then the breath gasped from my body, as I was plucked up and lifted through the rain-drizzling air. Above me the door in the hemisphere was open—a mouth growing larger as I was brought toward it.

I was expecting the lapse into unconsciousness which had occurred in my first encounter with a Tripod, outside the Chateau de la Tour Rouge, but it did not happen. Later I understood why. The Tripods had a means of doing this, but they used it only on the un-Capped, who might panic and struggle. There was no need for such restraint with those who had learned to worship them. The tentacle put me inside and released me, and I could take in my surroundings.

The hemispheres were some fifty feet across the base, but the part we were in was much smaller, an irregularly shaped cell about seven feet high. The outer wall with the door was curved, and had portholes on either side, covered with what seemed to be very thick glass. The remaining walls were straight, but the side ones sloped inward, so that the interior wall was shorter than the external. There was another door there, I saw, but it was closed.

There were no furnishings of any kind. I ran my fingernails over the metal and found it hard but satiny in texture. There were six in my group, and I had been the fifth to be taken. The last one was brought in, and the door closed, a raised round flap coming down to make a tight seal. I looked at the faces of my companions. They showed some confusion, but excitement and exaltation as well, which I did my best to copy. No one spoke, which was a help. I would not have known what to say, or how to say it.

Silence for endless minutes; then, abruptly, the floor tilted. The embarkation must have been completed. Our journey to the City had begun.

The motion was extremely odd. The three legs of the Tripods were attached to a circumferential ring beneath the hemispheres. At their points of attachment and where the legs jointed, there were segments which could lengthen and shorten as the legs shifted relative to each other. There was also an arrangement of springs between the ring and the hemisphere which compensated for much of the remaining jolting. What was left, after the tilt when the Tripod started to march, was a mild rocking movement. It was a little nauseating at first, but one rapidly grew accustomed to it.

The Tripods could travel as easily in one direction as another by reason of their three-legged symmetry, but at present the section we were in was at the front. We crowded to the portholes, and looked out.

Ahead, a little to our right, was the hill with the ancient semicircle of stone steps; behind it, the town where, the night before, we had feasted.

Beyond that again was the dark ribbon of the great river. We were going slightly north of east, heading toward it. The countryside beneath us was blurred and wet, but the actual rain had stopped and there was a patch of brightness in the cloud where the sun might be. Everything was small and far away. The fields and houses and cattle seen in the valley below from the Tunnel had been tinier, but that panorama had been fixed, unchanging. Here, change was continual. It was like being in the belly of a huge low-flying bird, flapping its way across the landscape.

Remembering the Tripods whose feet had served as boats, I wondered if these might do so, too, on reaching the river, but they did not. The forward leg sent up a fount of spray as it broke the surface, and the others followed. The Tripod crossed the riverbed as a horseman would have forded the stream below my father's mill at Wherton. On the other side, it changed direction, turning south. There was open country, and then desolation.

Beanpole and I had seen something of this brooding ruin of one of the great-cities on our way north—the river had flowed for miles between its black, unpromising shores. But from this high vantage point, one saw so much more. It stretched eastward from the river, a dark and ugly mass of destroyed buildings and broken roads. Trees had grown among them, but to a lesser extent than in the great-city we had crossed on our journey south to the White Mountains. This place seemed to be vaster, and uglier. I saw no remains of broad avenues and concourses, no sense, here, that our ancestors, before the Tripods came, had lived lives of order and beauty. But there was an awareness of might and power, and I wondered again how they could have been defeated—how we, a handful of shattered remnants, could hope to succeed where they had failed.

One of the others saw the City first, cried out, and we jostled each other to look. It rose beyond the edge of the ruins, a ring of dull gold standing against the gray of the horizon, surmounted and roofed in by an enormous bubble of green-tinged crystal. The Wall was more than three times as high as the Tripods, smooth and unbroken. The whole place, although resting solidly on the earth, seemed strangely unconnected with it. Some distance from the point for which we were making, a river bubbled up from under the shield of gold, and flowed away toward the mother river behind us. The eye, following its course, could almost imagine that the City was not there at all—that if one looked hard enough the illusion would vanish, and there would be just the river running through ordinary fields. But it did not vanish. The Wall rose higher as we approached, becoming more awful and forbidding.

The sky grew lighter. From one instant to the next, the sun broke through the mask of cloud. Sunlight glistened on the ramparts—was reflected from the crystal roof. It was a great band of gleaming gold, on which flashed a titanic emerald. And I saw a narrow slit of darkness, that widened. A door opened in the seamless wall. The first of the Tripods marched through.

What happened as our Tripod entered the City was something for which I was completely unprepared. I felt as though I had been struck a savage blow, but a blow which contrived to hit me in every part of my body at the same time, a blow from the front, from behind, most of all from above, smashing me down. I staggered and fell, and saw my companions do the same. The floor of the compartment pulled us, as though it were a magnet and we were flakes of iron. I struggled to rise, and I realized it was not a blow, but something different. All my limbs had turned to lead. It was an effort to raise my arm, even to twitch a finger: I strained, and stood up. I was carrying a tremendous burden on my back. Not on my back alone—on every square inch of bone and muscle in my body.

The others followed suit. They looked puzzled and frightened, but they still did not look unhappy. After all, whatever the Tripods wished on them was good: it must be. There was dim green light. It was as though one were very far down in a thick forest, or in a cave under the sea. I tried to make sense of it all, but could not. The weight on my body bowed my shoulders. I straightened myself up, but felt them sag again.

Time passed, and we waited. There was silence and heaviness and greenness. I tried to concentrate on what must be the most important thing—that we had achieved our first objective and were inside the Tripods' City. One must have patience. It was not, as Julius had pointed out, my most outstanding quality, but I had to command it now. Waiting would have been easier without the dimness and the crushing weight. It would have been a relief to say something, anything, but I dared not. I shifted my feet, seeking an easier stance, but not finding one.

I had been looking at the door on the inner wall, but it was the other which opened, swinging back and up with a faint whirring noise. There was still nothing to be seen outside—just a high dim green. A tentacle came in, and lifted one of my companions out. I realized that it must be able to see, independently of the hemisphere. Might it not still be that the Tripods themselves were sentient—that we were the captives of living and intelligent machines? The tentacle returned. This time it took me.

It was like a hall—long and narrow but of enormous size, probably eighty feet high and two or three times that in length. I saw that it was a kind of stable for Tripods—against one wall a long row of them stretched away into the green dusk, faintly illumined by hanging globes that gave a dim lemon-green light. Their hemispheres rested close against the wall, far above us. Those in which we had traveled were unloading their human cargo. I saw Fritz, but did not speak to him. We had agreed that no contact should be attempted until the first stage, whatever it proved to be, was safely over. One by one, the others joined us. At last the tentacles hung limp and inactive. A voice spoke.

This, too, sounded as though it might have been the voice of a machine. It was deep and toneless, echoing and booming in the vast space. The words were in the German language that we knew.

"Humans, you have the privilege, the high honor, to have been chosen as servants of the Masters. Go where the blue light shines. In the place to which it leads you, you will find fellow-slaves who will instruct you in what you are to do. Follow the blue light."

It had come on while the voice was speaking, a light that glowed deep blue in the base of the wall by which the Tripods were standing. We walked toward it, or staggered, rather, against the drag of this leaden weight which pulled us down. And the air was hotter, I thought, than it had been inside the Tripod, and clammy with it, like the moments before summer thunder. The light was above an open door, admitting us to a small room, much the same size as that in the Tripod, but of more regular shape. The door closed when we were all in. There was a click and another whirr, and suddenly the weight was even greater, seeming to drag my stomach down with it in a swoop of nausea. This lasted several seconds, and was followed by a brief sensation of lightness. The whirring stopped, the door opened, and we walked out into another room.

This also was large, although modest-seeming after the Hall of the Tripods, but of more conventional proportions. There was the same lemon-green glow from lamps which studded the walls. (Their light, I saw, did not flicker in the way our lamps did.) I had a confused impression of rows of tables, benches rather. And of half-naked old men.

They were the ones who, the voice said, were to instruct us. They wore only shorts, reminding me of men who worked in the harvest fields, but there was no other resemblance. The greenish light tricked the eyes, but even so I could see that their skins were an unhealthy pallid color. They came, one to each of us, and I followed my particular guide to the benches. A little pile of articles was laid out there.

Most of them were self-explanatory. There

were two pairs of shorts, like the ones our instructors were wearing, two pairs of socks, two pairs of shoes. No, one pair of shoes and one of sandals, the latter, I was told, for indoor wear. But there was also a device which baffled me. My guide explained it in a tired voice, with a South German accent.

"You must put this on before you go through the airlock, and wear it always while you breathe the Masters' air. In the house of your own Master you will have a room, in which to eat and sleep, where you will not need it, but otherwise it must never be removed. The air of the Masters is too powerful for such as we. If you go into it without protection, you will die."

It was like glass in that one could see through it, but different to the touch. Even the thicker part, which fitted over the head and rested on the shoulders, would yield a little when one pressed it, and it tapered to a thin stuff that molded itself to the body. There was a belt which went around the chest, high under the arms, and could be tightened to hold the helmet on firmly. On either side of the neck were pouches holding a dark green sponge-like material. These had a network of fine holes, on both outside and inside, admitting air. The sponges, it seemed, could filter out the part of the Masters' air which was too strong for their slaves to breathe. My instructor pointed to it.

"This must be changed every day. Your Master will supply you with new ones."

"Who is my Master?" I asked.

It was a foolish question. He stared at me blankly.

"Your Master will choose you."

I reminded myself that my policy was to lie low and say nothing, observing not questioning. But there was one thing I could not avoid asking.

"How long have you been in the City?"

"Two years."

"But you're not . . ."

The remnants of pride broke through the heavy dullness of his voice. He said, "I won the Thousand Meters at the Games, less than a month after I was Capped. No one from my province had ever done that before."

I stared at him, at the slumped tired body, the worn, sick-looking flesh, with horror. He was no more than two years older than I was, perhaps less.

"Change into these clothes." His voice was once more blank and expressionless. "Throw your old ones on that pile."

I took off my scarlet champion's belt. "What about this?"

"Put it with the rest," he said. "You do not need it in the City."

We dressed in our new clothes, putting the

articles we did not require immediately into a small bag which we were given, and fastened on our masks. Then we were marshaled along the room and through a door into another smaller one. The door closed behind us, and I saw there was an identical one on the opposite side. There was a hissing sound and I could feel a breeze over my feet and realized that air was being drawn into a grille that ran along the base of the wall. But air was also coming in, from another grille just above head level. I could feel it, and after a time I thought I could *see* it—thicker, greener in the green light. In some strange way the air was being changed in this room, the ordinary kind being replaced by that which the Masters breathed. It continued for several minutes. Then the hissing stopped, the door in front opened, and we were told to walk out.

It was the heat that struck me first. I had thought it was hot enough inside the Tripod and in the outer rooms of the City, but that was mild in comparison with the furnace-blast that I now encountered. And yet not a furnace-blast, because the air was damp as well as hot. Sweat started out all over my body but particularly on my head, encased in its hard transparent cover. It trickled down my face and neck to the place, high on my chest, where the belt trapped it against my skin. I drew in gulping breaths of hot, stifling air. I felt weak, and the weight dragged me down. My knees started to buckle. One of my companions fell, and then a second and a third. Two of them struggled back to their feet in a moment or two, the third lay still. I thought of helping him, but remembered my resolution not to take a lead in anything. I was glad of the excuse to do nothing. Keeping myself from falling or fainting was difficult enough.

Gradually I became a little more accustomed to things, and could look at what lay in front of us. We had come out on a kind of ledge, and the main thoroughfares of the City lay below us. It was an eye-wrenching confusion. None of the roads were straight, and few of them were level; they dipped and rose and curved between the buildings, and were lost in the dim green distance. The City seemed even vaster inside than it had from the porthole of the Tripod, but I had an idea that was because of the thicker, greener air. One could not see very far with any clarity. The crystal dome that covered everything was invisible from here: the green dusk seemed to stretch endlessly.

The buildings astonished me, too. They were in different shapes and sizes but of one general form: the pyramid. Immediately below our ledge I saw a number of squat, broad-based pyramids, farther off there were thinner, more tapering constructions that rose to differing heights, the smallest seeming almost as high as the ledge and others even taller. There were what looked like windows in them, triangular in shape, but dotted about the walls in no kind of pattern that I could understand. It tired my eyes to look at them.

Strange carriages moved along the ramps. These, too, broadly speaking, were pyramids, but resting on one side rather than on the base, which in this case formed the rear. The top parts were of a transparent material like our helmets, and I could see figures in them, but only very indistinctly. Other figures moved, on the spaces between the buildings and on the ledges which jutted from them at irregular intervals. They were of two kinds, one much smaller than the other. Although, at this distance, one could not make out particular features, it was obvious that one kind were the Masters, the other their human slaves. Because the smaller creatures moved slowly, as though dragging heavy weights, while the larger ones moved lightly and quickly.

One of our instructors said, "Behold. These are the dwellings of the Masters."

His voice, though muffled, was reverential. (Beneath the pouches with the sponges there were small metal devices. These, I found, carried sounds through the mask. The sounds were distorted, but to this, as to other things, one grew accustomed in time.) He raised a pointing hand, in the direction of one of the nearer pyramids.

"And there is the Choosing Place. Let us go down."

• • •

We made our slow and staggering way down a spiral ramp, whose steepness threw an extra aching strain on the muscles of our legs, causing falls now and then. (The boy who had fainted up on the ledge had revived and was with us. He was the one who had beaten Beanpole in the Long Jump, the gingery freckle-faced lad who had managed to put that extra effort into his final jump. He would not jump far here.) The heat, too, continued to drain our strength away, and the sweat, running down, formed an unpleasant puddle at the base of the mask. I wanted desperately to wipe it away, but of course that was impossible. To do so I would have had to take the mask off and, as I had been warned, this meant death in the air which the Masters breathed.

I had still not seen the Masters close enough for them to be anything but a blur. But, at least, one problem was solved. The Tripods were not themselves the enemy but merely machines which transported the Masters through the world outside the City. I did not see how this would help Julius and the others much, but it was information. Presumably I would learn more as time went by. After that, all Fritz and I needed to discover was a way of making our escape. All! I could have laughed at the thought, but lacked the energy. And I had to remember my role, of course, as one of the Capped, a chosen and willing slave.

The ramp led into one of the squat pyramids, about halfway up from the base. Inside there was light from dozens of lemon-green globes which hung at varying heights from the ceiling. If anything, the light was brighter than the dusk outside. We were taken down a curving corridor to a long room with a pointed ceiling. Along one side there was a row of open-fronted cubicles, their sides made of the hard glass-like substance. Each of us, we were told, was to go into one of these. After that, we were to wait. The Masters would come in due course.

We waited a long time. For the others, I imagine, it was easier. Being filled with the desire, above all things, to serve the Masters, would give them patience. Fritz and I had no such comfort. He was in a cubicle some ten away from mine, and I could not see him. I could see those on either side of me and, dimly, the two or three after that. I was filled increasingly with tension and apprehension, but knew I must not show it. There was discomfort also. Most of us were sitting or lying on the floor to help relieve the drag on our limbs. Lying was best, except for the sweat which had pooled inside the mask and, uncomfortable anyway, was intolerable if head and shoulders were not upright. By now, also, I was dreadfully thirsty, but there was nothing to drink and no means of drinking in any case. I wondered if they could have forgotten us—if we were to be left here until we died of thirst and exhaustion. Presumably we were of some value to them, but it would not be much. We could very easily be replaced.

I sensed rather than heard it at first, but it grew into a ripple of sound, spreading along the cubicles to my right—a sound of awe and wonder. I knew then that the moment had come, and craned my neck to see. They had entered the room from the far end, and were approaching the cubicles. The Masters.

For all the discomfort and fatigue, and fears as to what might happen, the first impulse I had was to laugh. They were so grotesque! They stood much taller than a man, nearly twice as tall, and were broad in proportion. Their bodies were wider at the bottom than the top, four or five feet around I thought, but tapered upward to something like a foot in circumference at the head. If it *was* the head, for there was no break in the continuity, no sign of a neck. The next thing I noticed was that their bodies were supported not on two legs but three, these being thick but short. They had, matching them, three arms, or rather tentacles, issuing from a point about halfway up their bodies. And their eyes— I saw that there were three of those, too, set in a flattened triangle, one above and between the other two, a foot or so below the crown. In color the creatures were green, though I saw that the shades differed, some being dark, the green tinged with brown, and others quite pallid. That, and the fact that their heights varied to some extent, appeared to be the only means of telling one from another. I felt it was a poor one.

Later I was to discover that, as one grew accustomed to them, identification was easier than I had expected. The orifices which were their mouths, and nose, and ears, varied too—in size, in shape a little, and in their relationship with each other. They were connected by a pattern of wrinkles and creases which one learned to know and recognize. At first impact, though, they were faceless, almost completely uniform. It sent a shiver of quite a different fear down my spine when one of them, stopping before me, spoke.

"Boy," he said, "stand up."

I thought the words issued from the mouth—which I judged the lower of the two central orifices to be—until I saw that it was the upper one which was quivering and open while the other remained closed and still. With the Masters, I was to discover, the organs of breathing and eating were not connected, as men's are: they spoke as well as breathed through one, ate and drank only through the lower, larger opening.

I stood up, as I was bid. A tentacle came toward me, touched me lightly and then more firmly on the arm. It ran along my flesh, like a snake, but clammily, lacking the dry smooth texture of a snake. I repressed a shudder.

"Move about," he said. The voice was cold, flat, not loud but penetrating. "Walk, boy."

I began to walk around the narrow confines of the cubicle. I thought of a horse sale I had seen once at Winchester—men feeling the muscles of the beasts, watching them parade around the ring. We did not need to be paraded; we could parade ourselves. The Master stood in front of me critically while I made several circuits of the cell. Then, with no other word or comment, he moved on. I stopped walking, and let myself slump back into a sitting position.

They traveled fast on those stumpy legs, bouncing off the ground with an up-and-down rhythmic motion. They were clearly vastly stronger than we were, to make so light of this leaden City. They could also, when they really wanted to get somewhere fast, spin along like tops, the three legs whirling them round and round and at the same time forward, with yards between each foot touching the ground. I suppose it was their version of running.

The Choosing went on. Another Master came to inspect me, and another. The boy in the next stall was taken: a Master ordered him to follow and he obeyed. They disappeared in the throng. Some Masters examined me more closely than others, but all moved on. I wondered if they were suspicious—if something in my behavior were not quite right. I also wondered what would happen if I were not chosen at all. It was known that no one returned from the City. In that case . . .

This particular alarm, I discovered, was unnecessary. Those who were not chosen as personal servants went into a general pool. But I did not know that at the time, and was aware of the stalls emptying around me. I saw Fritz go past, following a Master. We looked at each other, but gave no sign. A Master came up to my cubicle, stared at me for a moment, and went on, without speaking.

Their numbers had thinned, as well as ours. I sat on the floor miserably. I was tired and thirsty, my legs were aching, and the skin of my chest and shoulders was beginning to sting from the salt of my sweat. I leaned my back against the transparent wall, and closed my eyes. So I did not see the new Master who came, only heard his voice, commanding me.

"Get up, boy."

I thought it was a lighter voice than the others had been. I struggled to my feet, and looked at him.

Physically, he seemed to be shorter than average, and he was also darker in color. The

tinge of brown in the dark green was quite
marked. He stared down at me, the skin wrin-
kling between his eyes, and ordered me to show
my paces. I summoned my strength and moved
as briskly as I could; perhaps I had been too
lethargic for the others.

I was told to stop, and did so. The Master
said, "Come nearer."

As I moved toward him, a tentacle snaked
out and wrapped around my left arm. I gritted
my teeth. A second tentacle stroked appraisingly
along my body, assessing my legs, reaching up to
wind more closely around my chest in a grip that
forced breath from my lungs, then withdrew.
The voice said:

"You are a strange one, boy."

The words, summing up my chief fear, petrified me. I stared ahead at the featureless column
of the monster. There was almost certainly something I should be doing, showing. Excitement—
happiness at the prospect of being allowed to
serve one of these absurd and disgusting creatures? I tried to act out that mood. But the
Master was speaking again.

"How did you become a champion at the
Games—in which of your human sports?"

"Boxing . . ." I hesitated. "Master."

"You are small," he said. "But strong, I think,
for your size. Which part of the land do you
come from?"

"From the south, Master. Tirol."

"A mountain land. They are hardy ones, who come from the high parts."

He fell silent then. The tentacle that still held my left arm released it and dropped back. The three eyes stared at me. Then the voice said, "Follow me, boy."

I had found my Master; or he, rather, had chosen his slave.

Seven

My Master's Cat

I was fortunate in my Master.

He led me to his carriage, which was in a line
of others outside the building, showed me into it,
and drove us away. The driving would be one of
my duties, he explained. (It was not difficult.
They were moved by an invisible power that
came from below the ground. There was little to
do in the way of steering, and some device in the
machine made collisions impossible.) I saw that
some of the Masters with newly acquired slaves
were already forcing them to learn this skill, but
mine did not because he saw that I was tired and
distressed. The carriage ran on very many small
wheels, set beneath one face of a pyramid, the

driver having a seat in the pointed front part for controlling it. My Master drove it to the place where he lived, in toward the center of the City.

On the way I examined my surroundings. It was hard to make sense of the place—buildings and streets and ramps were at the same time very much like one another and confusingly different, their construction either unplanned or following a plan I could not begin to understand. Here and there I saw small areas which I supposed were meant for gardens. They were mostly triangular in shape, and filled with water, out of which grew strange plants of various colors—I saw red, brown, green, blue—but all somber. They all had the same general shape, too: a squatness at the base which tapered with height. Many of the garden pools had mists rising from them, and in some I saw Masters, moving slowly about or standing, like trees themselves, rooted in the water.

My own Master lived in a tall pyramid overlooking a large garden pool. It was five-sided but looked more like one of the triangles of which the Masters seemed to be so fond since three of the sides were shorter than the others and formed almost a straight line. We left the carriage outside the door—I looked back and saw the ground open under it and take it in—and went into the building. At the center we entered a moving room, like the one that had taken us from the Hall of the Tripods. My stomach lurched as it whirred, but this time I understood what was happening—that the room was moving upward and we with it. We came out in a corridor and I trudged along in the Master's wake to the door which was the entrance to his home.

There was much that I only understood later, of course. The pyramid was divided into homes for the Masters. Inside there was a smaller pyramid, completely enclosed by the outer one, which was used for storerooms, the place where the carriages were kept, the communal place for slaves, and so on. The homes were in the outer section, and one could tell a Master's importance in the City from the position of his home. Most important was the one right at the top—the pyramid on top of the pyramid. Next came the two triangular homes immediately below, and after that the homes at the corners of the pyramid, in descending order. My Master was only moderately important. His home was on a corner, but nearer the base than the apex.

At first sight of the City, with all these towering peaks, I had thought the number of the Masters must be fantastically great. At closer quarters, I realized that the impression had been to some extent misleading. Everything was on a far bigger scale than the human one to which I was accustomed. The homes, in particular, were spacious, the rooms being large and very high, twenty feet or more.

From the corridor, one came into a passage with several doors. (The doors were circular, and worked on the same principle as the one in the Tripod—a section swung inward and upward when a thing like a button was touched. There were no locks or bolts.) In one direction, the passage turned through a right angle at the end, and eventually issued into the most important part of the home: the triangular room that looked out from the building. Here the Master ate and relaxed. In the center of the floor there was a small circular garden pool, its surface steaming from extra heat provided beneath it, which was his favorite spot.

But I was not shown this right away. The Master took me along the passage in the opposite direction. It ended in a blank wall, but there was a door on the right a little before that. The Master said, "This is your refuge, boy. There is an airlock inside—that is a place where air is changed—and beyond that you can breathe without the mask. You will sleep and eat there, and you may stay there, or in the communal place, at times when I do not require your service. You may rest for a while now. In due course, a bell will ring. Then you must fix your mask on again, go back through the airlock, and come to me. You will find me in the window-room, which is at the end of the passage."

He turned and glided away, light on his stumpy feet, along the broad high passage. I understood that I had been dismissed, and pressed the button on the door in front of me. It opened and I stepped through, and automatically the door closed behind me. There was a hissing, and I felt the pull of the air current on my ankles as the Masters' air was drawn out and replaced by human. It did not take long, but it seemed like an age before the door on the opposite side opened, and I could step through. My fingers were tearing at the fastener of the belt that secured the mask as I did so.

I did not think that I could have supported the stifling confinement, with my own sweat pooling on my chest, for much longer, but later I found that I had been lucky. Fritz had been kept for several hours, being instructed in his duties, before he was allowed to find relief. My Master's consideration was apparent in other ways. The room set aside for the servant was small in floor area, but had the same towering height as the rest of the home. In this case the Master had had an intermediate floor constructed, with a ladder leading up to it. My bedroom was up there, whereas usually the bed had to be fitted into the limited living space.

Other than that there was a chair, a table (both of the simplest kind), a chest with two drawers, a cupboard for storing food, and a small toilet section. It was bare, and ugly. There was none of the extra heat, which the Master's rooms had, but no way of cooling, either, nor of freshening. One sweltered, the only alleviation being in the toilet section, where there was a device for spraying water on one's body. The water was lukewarm, both for that and for drinking, but cooler at least than the surrounding air. I let it play over me for a long time, and washed and changed my clothes. The air made the clean ones damp before I had put them on: no clothes were ever dry inside the City.

In the cupboard, I found food, in packets. It was of two kinds, a sort of biscuit to be eaten dry and some crumbling stuff to be mixed with the warm water from the tap. Neither had much taste, and they never varied. They were made by machines, somewhere in the City. I tried a little of the biscuit, but I found I was not hungry enough yet to eat it. Instead I hauled myself wearily up the ladder, a straining effort in this City of Lead, and dropped onto the bare hard bed that awaited me. There were no windows, of course, to my quarters, but a globe of green light in each, turned on and off by a button. I pressed the button, fell into darkness and oblivion, and dreamed I was back in the White Mountains, telling Julius that the Tripods were made of paper, not metal, and that one could chop their legs off with an axe. But in the middle of telling him, there was a savage clangor in my ears. I awoke with a start, and realized where I was, and that I was being summoned.

Knowing nothing of conditions in the City, Fritz and I had not been able to make any specific plans for finding each other, though naturally we were anxious to do so as soon as possible. When I contemplated the size and complexity of the place, despondency overcame me; I did not see how we could ever hope to make contact. There were, plainly, thousands of Masters in the City. If every one of these had a servant . . .

In one way it was less difficult than I had thought; in others, more. To start with, each Master did not have a servant. It was a privilege reserved for those of a certain rank, probably less than a thousand in all, and not all availed themselves of the right. There was a movement in opposition to the presence of humans in the City. It was based on a fear, not that the slaves might revolt, because no one doubted their docility, but that the Masters, in accepting the personal service of other creatures, were somehow weakened and degraded. The total of humans, drawn from the Games and from other selection procedures in other places, was probably no more than five or six hundred.

But between this five or six hundred, means

of communication were extremely limited. There was, apart from the individual refuges inside one's Master's apartment, a communal place for slaves in each of the residential pyramids. There, in a larger, but still windowless room, it was possible to meet and talk, with a number flashing in a box on the wall to tell you when your Master required your return. One could not go to a communal place in other buildings without running the risk of being absent when the call came. And the risk was never taken, not through fear of punishment but because, to the Capped, it was unthinkable that they should fail the Master in any way.

We might meet on the street, sent on errands by our different Masters, but the odds were against that. It soon seemed obvious that the only real chance of discovering each other lay in our Masters both attending the same function, at which (as was true of most) there was a restroom for slaves.

There were a number of such functions, I discovered. The one of which my Master was fondest was one in which they rooted themselves in a pool inside a pyramid, while in the center a group of them used their tentacles to agitate devices which rippled the water and shook the air and at the same time sent out wild sounds, which my Master found pleasurable but which to me seemed hideous. At another, the Masters spoke to each other in their own language, full of whistling and grunting sounds; in a third, Masters on a raised stage hopped and whirled about in what I supposed was meant to be a dance.

To all these, at different times, I accompanied him, and went eagerly to the restroom, to shower and dry myself, and perhaps eat a piece of the monotonous biscuit or, at least, lick one of the salt sticks with which we were provided. And to hunt among the other slaves for Fritz. But again and again I drew a blank, and I began to think it was hopeless. I knew that not all the Masters enjoyed these things, just as there were events to which my Master did not choose to go. It was beginning to seem that we had had the bad luck to be chosen by Masters whose interests were very different.

In fact, this was true. My Master was fondest of things that stemmed from the mind and imagination, Fritz's of those which exercised and demonstrated the body. Fortunately, though, there was one event which had an almost universal appeal. They called it the Sphere Chase.

It took place, at regular intervals, in the Sphere Arena. This was a great open space, in the shape, naturally, of a triangle, near the center of the City. It was covered with some reddish substance and there were seven posts, perhaps thirty feet high, each with a basket-like contraption at the top. Three of these were set at the points of the triangle, three midway between the points, and the seventh in the center.

That is as much, really, as I can describe which makes sense. I think what happened in the arena was a kind of game, but if so it was not like any game that men play. Small Tripods, standing not more than twenty feet high, issued out from a place below ground behind one point of the triangle, performed a complicated marching about for a time, and then started chasing each other. After a while, in the course of this chase, one or more golden spheres would appear in the air between the probing point of the Tripods' tentacles. This was generally greeted by a loud booming noise from the Masters who were watching all around in terraced seats, and the booming would increase as the chase and pursuit continued with the golden ball flashing and tossing between them. At some stage, the sphere would be flung over or around one of the baskets on top of the poles, and eventually would light in the basket when there would be a great coruscating flash, a noise like a clap of thunder, and the booming from the spectators would be punctuated with wails and howls. This was much intensified when it happened to be the center pole's basket that was hit, both as to flash and thunder, and what I imagine was applause. Then the chase began all over again, and a new ball was created.

The small Tripods, I found, were occupied by one or, at the most, two Masters. It seemed that much skill was involved in the Sphere Chase, and those who were best at it were greatly honored. On that last bit of the trek that Henry and Beanpole and I had made to the White Mountains, when the two Tripods came across us out in the open but took no notice—then, too, there had been the golden ball flashing against the blue sky. I realized that the Masters driving those Tripods must have been Sphere Chasers, practicing for the next Chase and too engrossed to concern themselves with anything else. It represented a weakness in the Masters: trivial, perhaps, but any sign of fallibility was something to rejoice at.

The other good thing was that the Sphere Chase was the means of finding Fritz, after weeks of fruitless searching. I accompanied my Master to his seat in that side of the Triangle reserved for the superior ones, and hurried—which meant a lumbering rather than a dragging walk—down to the restroom beneath. It was larger than any other communal room I had seen, but crowded for all that—there must have been a couple of hundred slaves in it. I pulled off my mask, placed it in one of the lockers along the wall near the entrance, and went looking for him. He was at the far end, in the queue for the salt sticks which we sucked to replace the salt we lost through our continual sweating. He saw me and nodded, and brought two salt sticks over to where I stood, as far removed from the others as possible.

I was shocked by the sight of him. This was a life, I knew, which would drag anyone down, if only by reason of the relentless clammy heat and the constant drag on bone and muscle. Many of the humans I had met were in a pitiful state, old and enfeebled long before their time. I was conscious in myself that, although I was learning to live with the heat and weight, and to husband my energy, gradually my strength was ebbing. But the change in Fritz was far beyond expectation.

We had all lost weight but he, who had been tall and well-built, seemed, in proportion, to have lost much more than I. His ribs showed painfully through the flesh of his chest, and his face was gaunt. He had the stooped posture that one saw in those who had been a year or more in the City. I saw something else, too, with horror: a pattern of angry marks across his back. I knew that some of the Masters beat their human servants, for carelessness or stupidity, using a thing like a fly whisk, which burned the flesh where it touched. But Fritz was not stupid and would not be careless.

Giving me the salt stick, he said in a low voice, "The most important thing is to make arrangements for future meetings. I am at 71

Pyramid 43. It would be better to meet there, if you have an easy Master."

I said, "Where is that? I still can't find my way about."

"Near the . . . No. Tell me where you are."

"19 Pyramid 15."

"I can find that. Listen. My Master goes to a garden pool almost every day, regularly at two seven. He stays for a period. I think there's time enough to get to your pyramid. If you can manage to get down to your communal place . . ."

"I'll do that, easily."

"I'll say I'm the slave of a visiting Master."

I nodded. We used Masters' time in the City, not human. The day was divided into nine periods, and each period was divided into ninths. It was made difficult by the fact that the day started with sunrise, and so changed continually. Two seven was approximately noon. My Master, too, often went to a garden pool around then. Even if he did not, I could keep some small errand until that time.

"Your Master," I said, "—is he very bad?"

Fritz shrugged. "Bad enough, I think. I have nothing to compare with."

"Your back . . ."

"He enjoys that."

"Enjoys!"

"Yes. At first I thought it was because I was

doing things wrong, but it is not so. He finds reasons. I howl and shriek a lot, which pleases him. I have learned to howl louder, and it does not go on so long. What about your Master? I see that your back is unmarked."

"I think he is a good one."

I told Fritz something of my life, of the small signs of consideration I was given. He listened, and nodded.

"A very good one, I would say."

He related a few other things about his own life, from which it was plain that the whippings were far from being the only respect in which he suffered worse than I. In every way possible, his Master humiliated and persecuted and heaped impossible burdens on him. I was almost ashamed to have been so lucky. He did not dwell on this, though, but said, "Anyway, all that is not important. It is what we find out about the City that matters. We must exchange information with each other, so that what one learns the other knows. You tell me first what you have discovered."

"Very little so far. Practically nothing." I searched my brain for snippets, and retailed them to him. They were a meager collection. "That's all, I think."

Fritz had listened gravely. He said, "It all helps. I have found where the great machine is from which they get heat and light, and the means for making the carriages go. For making the City so heavy as well, probably. Ramp 914 leads off Street 11. It goes through a place with garden pools on either side, and then dips down into the earth. The machine is down there somewhere. I have not been able to go down yet—I am not sure if humans can go there—but I will try further.

"Also, I have found the place where water comes into the City. It is in Wall Sector 23. A river comes in below ground and passes through another machine which makes the water suitable for the Masters. I have been there, and will go again. It is a huge place and I cannot understand much about it yet. Then there is the Place of Happy Release."

"Of Happy Release?"

I had heard this phrase spoken once or twice by other slaves, but had no clue as to its meaning. Fritz said, "That is not far from here, along Street 4. It is the place where the slaves go when they know they are no longer strong enough to serve the Masters. I followed one, and saw it happen. There is a place where the slave stands, beneath a dome of metal. There is a flashing light, and he drops to the floor, dead. Then the floor on which his body is lying moves. It goes along, and a door opens, and there is a white-hot furnace inside, which burns the body away to nothing."

He went on to tell me what he had discovered about the other slaves in the City. They did not only come from the Games; in other countries they were selected in different ways, but always for youth and strength. The life in the City, even where the Masters, like mine, were tolerant, possibly kind, was one which killed them, slowly but surely. Some crumpled up and died almost at once; others lasted a year, two years. Fritz had met a slave who had been more than five years in the City, but he was exceptional. When the slave knew that death was on him, he went, of his own volition, to the Place of Happy Release, and died in the glad assurance that he had served the Masters to the utmost of his ability and the last atom of energy.

I listened carefully to all this. Now I was really ashamed. I had been thinking my life was hard, and had been treating this as an excuse for not doing anything much—in effect, I had been marking time, hoping to get in touch with Fritz and then think of what to do. He, with so much worse to suffer, had nevertheless been getting on with the task which we shared, and on which man's future might depend.

I asked him, "How did you manage to find all these things, if you can only get away during the two hours he spends at the garden pool? You could not get to them all in that time, surely."

"There is another Master with whom he has

twice spent a day. He is one of those who disapprove of slaves, and my Master leaves me behind. So I got out, and explored."

"If he had returned unexpectedly, or called you . . ."

There was a means in each home by which a Master could call his slave to come to him. Fritz said:

"I had thought of an excuse. He would beat me, of course, but I am used to it."

There had been an occasion when I had been left behind. I had spent the day resting, talking in the communal center; once I had gone out, but the confusion of streets and ramps and pyramids had depressed me, and I had come back. I felt myself flushing.

We had been talking apart from the others, but more and more slaves had been arriving from the arena above us, and the room was beginning to be crowded. Fritz said, "Enough now. 19 Pyramid 15. The communal place at about two nine. Good-bye, Will."

"Good-bye, Fritz."

Watching him lose himself in the throng of slowly moving slaves, I made a resolve—to go about my task more keenly, and with less self-pity.

The duties I had to perform for my Master were not in themselves particularly onerous. I had to tidy the home, prepare and serve his food, see to his bath, make his bed—that sort of thing. As far as food was concerned, preparation was easy enough, for it consisted of mixtures of differing texture and color (and flavor, too, I imagine), which came in transparent bags. Some needed to be mixed with water, but many of them were eaten just as they were. Serving was a different matter. Portions of the foods were put on a triangular dish and eaten in a certain order, and the placing and the ways in which they were laid out were important. I became good at this quite quickly, and was commended for it. It was a little more difficult than it seems, because there were dozens of patterns, not just one, which had to be learned.

He had a bath several times a day, in addition to visits to one of the garden pools and wallowings in the smaller pool in the window-room: all the Masters soaked themselves in water as often as they could. His private bath was next to the room in which he slept. Steps led up to it, and the bath itself was a hole in which he could put his body to be wholly submerged. The water was specially hot for this; it welled up from the bottom, boiling. I had to put in powders and oils which colored and scented the water, and lay out a number of strange brush-like devices with which he scrubbed himself.

The bed was upright, too, and of much the

same shape as the bath, but instead of the approach being by steps, it was up a spiral ramp—a fairly steep one, which it made me pant to climb. Inside was placed a sort of damp moss, and each day I had to remove the old and replace it with fresh from the bed cupboard. Although the moss looked light, it weighed heavy. I suppose this was the hardest of my tasks, as far as labor was concerned.

But apart from these, and other similar duties, there was another function which I found myself fulfilling: that of companionship. Except for the occasions on which they joined together to watch the Sphere Chase, or other forms of entertainment, the Masters led strangely solitary lives. They visited one another, but not often, and spent a good deal of their time in their homes alone. (Even in the garden pools, I noticed, they did not talk to each other much.) To some, though, this isolation came less easily than to others—to my own Master I suspected it did. A human slave to him was not merely someone to do various menial chores around the home, not merely a sign that he was of the rank that qualified him to own such a one, but someone who could listen to him talk. In my village at home, old Mrs. Ash had six cats and spent most of her day talking to one or the other of them. I was my Master's cat.

With the advantage, of course, of being a cat

who could talk back. He not only spoke to me of the things that happened to him (I could rarely make any sense out of them, and I never began to understand what work he did), but asked questions as well. He was curious about me, and about my life before winning at the Games and coming to the City. At first I was suspicious of his interest, but I quickly realized that it was innocent. So I told him all about the way I had lived as the son of a small dairy farmer in the Tirol—how I had driven the cows up to pasture in the high meadows at the beginning of the day and stayed with them until it was time to bring them back for milking in the evening. I invented brothers and sisters, cousins and uncles and aunts, a whole pattern of life which he accepted and seemed to take an interest in. When I was off-duty, I used to lie on my bed in my refuge and think of more lies to tell him: it was a way of passing the time.

Or had been until I realized how little I had been doing compared with Fritz. But when I said something about it to Fritz the following day when we met again in the communal place of my pyramid, he took a different view. He said, "You have been very lucky with that one. I had no idea any of the Masters spoke to us slaves, except to give orders. Mine does not, certainly. He beat me again this morning, but he did it in silence: I was the one who made a noise. Perhaps you can learn more from this than from exploring the City."

"If I asked questions, he would certainly be suspicious. The Capped do not pry into the wonders of the Masters."

"Not questions, as such. But perhaps you can lead him on. You say he talks about his own life, as well as asking you about life outside?"

"Sometimes. But it makes no sense. He has to use their words when he talks about his work because there are no human words for the things he is telling me about. A few days ago he was saying that he was feeling unhappy because during the zootleboot a tsutsutsu went into spiwis, and therefore it was not possible to izdool the shuchutu. At least, it sounded something like that. I saw no point in even trying to understand what it meant."

"If you keep on listening, it may make sense in time."

"I don't see how it can."

"It may, though. You must persevere, Will. Encourage him to talk. Does he use the gas bubbles?"

These were small rubbery spheres which could be stuck to the Master's skin, below the nose opening. When they were pressed by one of the Master's tentacles, a reddish-brown mist came out and rose slowly upward, encircling the Master's head.

I said, "He has one a day, sometimes two, when he is in the pool in the window-room."

"I think it does to them what strong drink does to men. Mine beats me harder after he has sniffed a gas bubble. Maybe yours will talk more. Take him another while he is in the pool."

I said doubtfully, "I doubt if it will work."

"Try, anyway."

He looked ill and exhausted. The welts on his back were bleeding slightly.

I said, "I'll try tomorrow."

And I did, but the Master waved me away. He asked me how many calves cows bore, and then mentioned that the pooshlu had strool-glooped. I did not seem to be getting very far.

Eight

The Pyramid of Beauty

When I had just about abandoned hope of getting any useful information out of the Master, he solved the problem for me himself. His work, whatever it was, took place in a squat pyramid about half a mile from the one in which he lived. I had to drive him there in the carriage, and stay in the communal place with the other slaves until he was ready to return. This would be after two periods (just over five human hours), and I used the time, as the other slaves did, to rest, and if possible sleep. One learned early in one's life in the City the overwhelming importance of conserving energy to the maximum degree possible. There were couches provided in this communal place. They were hard, and there were not enough to go around, but it was a luxury which was far from being universal, and I was grateful for it.

On this occasion I had been lucky enough to get a couch, and was lying on it drifting into sleep, when my arm was shaken. I asked hazily what was the matter, and was told that my number was flashing on the call-box, indicating that I was wanted. My first thought was that it was a trick to get me off the couch, which the other slave probably wanted for himself, and I said as much. But he insisted that it was true, and at last I roused myself to look, and saw that it was.

As I got my mask and prepared to put it on, I said, "I don't see how the Master can want me. It's only been three ninths. There must be a mistake."

The other had taken my place on the couch and was lying there prone. He said, "It may be the Sickness."

"What sickness?"

"It is something that happens with the Masters from time to time. They stay at home for two or three days, or even longer. It is more common with those like your Master who have brown in their skins."

I remembered that I had thought, that morning, that his skin was darker than usual. When I went to him in the outer room and made the customary deep bow of respect, I noticed that it was very much darker, the brown more pronounced and that his tentacles, even though at rest, were quivering slightly. He told me to drive him home, and I obeyed.

I thought, remembering human sickness, that he might want to go to bed, and realized that I had not yet changed his moss. He did not do that, though, but instead went into the pool in the window-room and squatted there, motionless and silent. I asked him if there was anything he needed, and he did not answer. So I went to the bedroom and got on with my work. I had just finished, and was putting the old moss into the cupboard in which it could be destroyed, when the bell rang for me.

He was still in the pool. He said, "Boy, bring me a gas bubble."

I did as I was told, and watched him place it between mouth and nose and press on it with a tentacle. The reddish-brown mist oozed out, like a liquid almost, and rose up. The Master breathed in deeply. This went on, with him taking breaths of it at intervals, until the bubble was empty. He tossed it away, for me to pick up, and called for another. This was unusual. He used it, and had me bring him a third. He started talking not long afterward.

It did not make much sense at first. I gathered he was talking about the Sickness. He spoke of the Curse of the Skloodzi, which seemed to be the name of his family or his race, or perhaps it was the name the Masters gave themselves. There was a lot about wickedness—I was not sure whether he meant his own or that of the Masters in general—but although he bemoaned it, I could not help feeling that he did so with a certain amount of satisfaction. The Sickness was a punishment for wickedness, and therefore had to be endured with stoicism. He flicked away the third empty gas bubble with his central tentacle, and told me to get a fourth, and to move faster this time.

The gas bubbles were in the room where the food was kept. I went to bring one, but when I returned to the window-room he was out of the pool. He said, his voice more distorted than usual, "I ordered you to move faster, boy."

Two of the tentacles gripped me, and held me in mid-air as easily as I might have held a kitten. He had not touched me since that first meeting in the Choosing Place, and I was more shocked than anything else. But shock was rapidly replaced by pain. The third tentacle whipped through the air and lashed my back. It was like being hit by a heavy length of rope. I jerked against the tentacles that held me, but it did no good. The lash came down again, and again. Now it felt more like a sapling than a rope that was striking me. I thought it would break my ribs, even perhaps my spine. Fritz had said that he cried out because he realized his Master wanted him to cry out. I supposed I ought to do the same, but I would not. I gritted my teeth, crushing a fold of skin between them and sending hot salty blood flowing inside my mouth. The beating went on. I had given up counting the blows; there were too many of them. And then there was a roaring in my ears, and oblivion.

I recovered to find myself lying on the floor. I moved slightly, and there was pain again: my body seemed to be one long bruise. I forced myself to get up. As far as I could tell, no bones were broken. I looked for the Master, and saw him squatting, silent and motionless, in the pool.

I was humiliated and angry, and aching all over. I limped from the room and took the passage round to my refuge. Once inside, I stripped off my mask, dried the sweat from my neck and shoulders, and hauled myself up the ladder to my bed. I realized as I did so that I had omitted the customary bow of reverence to the Master when I left the window-room. I had certainly not felt reverential toward him, but that was not the point. The essential thing was in every way to imitate the behavior of the truly Capped. It had been a slip, and could be a dangerous one. As I was thinking of this, the ringing of the bell hammered my nerve endings. My Master wanted me again.

Wearily I descended, put on my mask, and left the refuge. My mind was confused, and I did not know what to expect. The thought of another beating was uppermost, and I did not know how I was to endure it: it hurt even to walk. I was entirely unprepared for what did happen when I returned to the window-room. The Master was no longer in the pool but standing near the entrance. A tentacle seized me and lifted me. But instead of the lash for which I was vainly trying to prepare myself, there came, from the second tentacle, a gentle stroking gesture, a snake's soft writhing along my battered ribs. I was a kitten being cuddled now, after it had been chastised.

The Master said, "You are a strange one, boy."

I said nothing. I was being held awkwardly, with my head slightly lower than my body. The Master went on, "You did not make loud noises as the others have done. There is a difference in you. I saw it that first day in the Choosing Room."

What he said petrified me. I had not realized, though I suppose I should have done, that the natural reaction of the Capped to being beaten would be to howl like children. Fritz had sensed this and behaved accordingly, but I had stupidly resisted through pride. And then had failed to make the bow of reverence afterward. I was terrified that the Master's next move would be to probe the Cap with the tip of his tentacle through the softer part of the mask. If he did, he would soon realize the difference between mine and the true Caps, which knit in with the living flesh. And then . . .

But instead he put me down. Belatedly I made the bow of reverence and, because of my soreness and stiffness, nearly overbalanced while doing it. The Master steadied me, and said, "What is friendship, boy?"

"Friendship, Master?"

"There is an archive in the City where those things your people call books are kept. I have studied some of them, being interested in your race. Some of the books are lies, but lies which seem like truth. Friendship is one of the things of which they tell. A closeness between two entities . . . that is a strange business to us Masters. Tell me, boy—in your life before you were chosen to serve, did you have such a thing? A friend?"

I hesitated, and said, "Yes, Master."

"Speak of him."

I talked of my cousin Jack, who had been my closest friend until he was taken to be Capped. I changed the details to the life I was supposed to have led, in the mountainous Tirol, but I described the way we had done things together, and the den which we had made outside the village. The Master listened attentively. He said finally:

"There was a link between you and this other human—a link that was voluntary, not forced by circumstances . . . so that you desired to be together, to talk with each other. Is this right?"

"Yes, Master."

"And it happens much with your people?"

"Yes, Master. It is a common thing."

He fell into a silence. It lasted a long time, and in the end I wondered whether he had forgotten about me, as sometimes happened, and whether I should take my leave, being careful to remember to bow. But as I was contemplating this, the Master spoke again.

"A dog. That is a small animal that lives with men?"

"Some do, Master. Some are wild."

"It has been stated, in one of the books that I saw, 'His only friend was his dog.' Can this be true, or is it one of the lies?"

"It can be true, Master."

"Yes," he said, "that is what I have thought." His tentacles described a small movement in the air which I had come to recognize as expressing satisfaction. Then one of them wrapped itself, but not roughly, around my waist.

"Boy," said the Master, "you will be my friend."

I was almost too astonished to think. I had

got it wrong, I saw. I was not a kitten, after all, in the Master's eyes. I was his puppy!

When I saw Fritz, and was able to tell him of what had happened, I expected him to find it funny, but he did not. He said seriously, "This is a wonderful thing, Will."

"What's wonderful about it?"

"The Masters seemed all alike at first, but I suppose men would to them. In fact, they differ a great deal. Mine is strange in one way, yours in another. But the strangeness of yours may help us to learn things about them, while with mine"—he forced a grin—"it is merely painful."

"I still dare not ask him things that the Capped would not ask."

"I am not so sure. You should have howled when he thrashed you, but it was because you didn't that he became interested in you. He said you were strange before he told you that you were to be his friend. They are not used to seeing free men, remember, and it would never occur to them that a human could be dangerous. I think you can ask him things, as long as the questions are general, and you keep making the bow of reverence at the right time."

"Perhaps you're right."

"It would be useful to find the archive where the books are. They had the Capped destroy all the books that held the knowledge of the ancients, but I suppose they would not have destroyed them here."

"I will try to find out."

"But go carefully," he warned. He looked at me. "Your task is not an easy one."

He was thinking, I felt, that he could have carried it out a good deal better than I; and I was inclined to agree with him. Where I had stubbornness and pride, he had a watchful endurance. He was looking ill, and had been badly beaten again that morning. The whip his Master used left marks which faded in about forty-eight hours, and these welts were fresh. He had once or twice been beaten with a tentacle, as I had been, and said that, although one ached for longer afterward, the beating itself was not so bad as with the whisk thing. I hated to think of what that must be like.

Fritz went on to tell me of his own latest discoveries. The most useful of these was that he had found a place where there were walls with pictures of stars at night, and the Masters could make these pictures move. In the same pyramid, there was a globe, almost as high as he was, turning on a spindle, and the globe's entire surface was a map. He had not wanted to seem too curious, but there was a part he had recognized as depicting the places which we knew: it showed the narrow sea across which Henry and I had come, the White Mountains far to the south, and the great river down which the *Erlkönig* had sailed. And on the map, at a point which he calculated as being roughly our present location, there was a golden button, which could only be the City.

As far as he could see, there were two other golden buttons on the globe, both well to the south of this one and situated far apart, one on the edge of a great continent to the east, the other on an isthmus between two continents to the west. They must also represent Cities of the Masters, which meant there were three in all, from which the world was ruled. A Master had come into the room at that stage, and Fritz had been forced to move on. But he planned to go back, and get the positions fixed more firmly in his head.

I still had nothing that seemed worthwhile to report. Except that I was to be my Master's puppy. He had said my task was not easy. In one sense, I saw, he was right. But in every other respect his was incomparably the harder. And he was the only one who seemed to be getting anywhere.

My Master's Sickness lasted for several days. He did not go to his place of work, and spent a lot of time squatting in the pool in the window-room. He breathed the gas bubbles a good deal, but did not beat me again. Occasionally he came out of the pool and picked me up and fondled me, and he also talked to me. Some of it was as incomprehensible as when he had talked about his work, but not all. I found one day, when the green dusk outside was fading as the sun, beyond the dome, slanted out of sight in the west, that he was talking about the Masters' conquest of the earth.

They had come in a vast ship that could move through the emptiness between the worlds, and the greater emptiness between the stars that warmed the worlds circling around them. This ship had been propelled at an unimaginable speed, almost as fast, he told me, as a sunbeam travels, but even so the journey had lasted many long years of time. (The Masters, I now realized, lived immensely longer than we did, for this one—and, I think, all the Masters in the City—had made that journey, and lived here ever since.) Theirs had been an expedition sent out with the purpose of finding worlds that their people could conquer and colonize, and an expedition that had many setbacks and disappointments. Not all stars had planets near them, and where they did these planets were usually unsuitable, for various reasons.

The world from which the Masters came was much larger than the earth, and hotter. Being larger, things on its surface weighed more. The Masters had found some worlds too small and others too big for their purpose, some too cold—being far removed from the central sun—and others too hot. Of the ten worlds circling our sun, ours was the only one that would do, and it had an atmosphere poisonous to them and a gravity too light. All the same, it was thought to be worth conquering.

So the great ship was made to go in a circle around the earth, as the moon does, and the Masters studied the world which they were to seize. It seems that the ancients had marvelous machines by which they could speak and show pictures at a distance, and the Masters were able to listen and watch without needing to come close enough for their ship to be seen. They stayed like this for many years, occasionally sending smaller ships nearer to examine things which were not shown on the distance-pictures, or not in sufficient detail. (Some of the ancients, my Master said, reported seeing these ships, but others did not believe them. This could not have happened with the Masters, but men had this strange thing called lying, in which they told of things that had not occurred, and therefore they did not trust each other.)

They recognized that in man they had an enemy who might be formidable. There were all these marvels, like the distance-pictures, there were the great-cities at the height of their glory and power, and there were other things, too.

Men had already begun to build ships that would take them across the emptiness. They had nothing like the ships of the Masters, but they had started, and they were learning fast. And they had weapons. One of these, from what he said, was of the nature of the iron eggs Beanpole had found in the Tunnel below the great-city; but as much more powerful as a bull compared to an ant. With one of these giant eggs, the Master told me, an area of land many miles in circumference could be scorched and blasted—one of the great-cities itself completely obliterated.

If they had brought their ship down to the earth, and made a bridgehead, that bridgehead would have been destroyed. They had to find a different method. The one they chose lay in a field of knowledge where they were even more advanced than star traveling—the understanding and control of the mind.

When, on the journey to the White Mountains, they had put the button under my arm by which the Tripods afterwards tracked us, and Henry had said that I must have known it was there, Beanpole had spoken of the man in the circus who could make people go to sleep and then obey his commands. I had once seen such a man with a traveling fair that came to Wherton. This sort of thing, and much, much more, was known to the Masters. They could, quite easily, put men to sleep and make them, even without the Caps, obey commands—for a time at least. But the problem still remained of getting men into a position where their power could be used. It is no good being able to make a rabbit pie, unless you can first catch your rabbit.

And they caught their rabbits with the ancients' own marvel: the distance-pictures. These pictures were sent out on invisible rays through the air, and turned back into pictures in millions on millions of homes all over the world. The Masters found a means of suppressing those rays at their source, and sending out in their place rays which made the pictures they wanted. There went with them other rays that made men's minds receptive. So they watched the pictures, and the pictures told them to go to sleep, and when they had gone to sleep, the pictures gave them their orders.

This control, as I have said, would wear off eventually, but it lasted for days, and the Masters made good use of the time. A hundred small ships landed, and men flocked to them as they had been told, and the Caps were put on their heads—by Masters at first, but later by men who had already been Capped. It was a process which grew as it went on. All that was needed was that there should be enough Caps, and there were. The plans had been well laid.

By the time those who had not watched the

pictures realized something of what was happening, it was almost too late to do anything about it. They were separate, isolated, while the others were working under the orders of the Masters, united in one purpose. And by the time the effect of the commands given by the distance-pictures wore off, enough men had been Capped to ensure that the Masters would not have any but scattered and ineffective opposition to face: one of the first things the Capped had done was to take control of the mighty weapons of the ancients. So it was possible for the parent-ship to come down to earth, and the first occupation base to be set up.

That was not quite the end, my Master told me. Some resistance continued. There were great ships on the sea, and ships that traveled under the sea; and some of these remained free for a time, and had weapons with which they could strike from half a world away. The Masters had to track them down, to destroy them, and one of the undersea ships survived for more than a year, and at the end of that time somehow located the main base, and sent one of the giant eggs through the air, to miss its target only by a narrow margin. In the attack though, it revealed its own position, so that the Masters could use a similar weapon of their own, and sink it.

On land, there was sporadic fighting for years, though steadily diminishing because all the time the number of the Capped grew while the number of the free diminished. The Tripods stalked the earth, guiding and helping their followers against bands of men whose weapons were puny, or nonexistent. In the end, there was peace.

I said, "So now all men are happy, having the Masters to rule and help them, and no more wars and wickedness."

It was an expected comment, and I tried to put as much enthusiasm as possible into it. The Master said, "Not quite all. Last year, a Tripod was attacked and the Masters in it killed when the poisonous air broke in on them."

I said, shocked, "Who could do that?"

One of his tentacles splashed water over him from the pool. He said, "Before you were Capped, boy, did you love the Masters as you do now?"

"Of course, Master." I hesitated. "Perhaps not quite as much. The Cap helps."

He moved a tentacle in a gesture which I knew to be a sign of agreement. He said, "The Caps are put on when the skull is near the end of its growing. There are some Masters who think now that it should be done earlier, because some humans, in the year or two before they are Capped, become rebellious and act against the Masters. This was known, but not thought important, because the Cap makes them good again. But it was boys like these who found old weapons that still had power, and used them in such a way that four of the Masters were killed."

Making a note of the fact that four was presumably a standard crew for a Tripod, I feigned a great shudder of horror, and said passionately, "Then of course boys must be Capped earlier!"

"Yes," the Master said. "I think that will happen. It means that the Capped will die sooner, and have pains in their heads because the Caps grip their skulls more tightly, but it is unwise to take risks, even small risks."

I said, "The Masters must not be endangered."

"On the other hand, there are some who think it does not matter because at last we are in sight of the Plan being achieved. When that happens, there will be no more need for Caps at all."

I waited, but he stayed silent. Greatly daring, I said, "The Plan, Master?"

He still did not reply, and I dared not press the question further. After perhaps half a minute, he said, "I have a night-feeling sometimes when I think of it. It is probably the Sickness, the Curse of the Skloodzi. What is goodness, boy, and what is wickedness?"

"Goodness lies in obeying the Masters."

"Yes." He slumped farther down in the steaming water of the pool, and wrapped his tentacles around him: I did not know what that gesture meant. "In a way, boy, you are lucky to wear the Cap."

I said fervently: "I know I am very lucky, Master."

"Yes." A tentacle unrolled and beckoned. "Come nearer, boy."

I went to the edge of the pool. The tentacle, slimy from the water, caressed me, and I did my best to disguise the repulsion I felt. He said, "I am glad of this friendship, boy. It helps with the Sickness, particularly. In this book of which I spoke, the human got things for his dog that his dog liked to have. Is there anything you wish, boy?"

I hesitated a moment, and said, "I like seeing the wonders of the City, Master. I would be happy to see more of them."

"That may be done." The tentacle, with a final pat, withdrew, and he began rising out of the pool. "Now I desire to eat. Prepare my table."

The following day the Sickness had abated, and the Master returned to his work. He gave me a thing to wear on my wrist and explained that anywhere in the City this would make a sound like many bees when he wanted me. I was to come to him then, but otherwise I could wander about: it was not necessary, for instance, that I should stay in the communal room of the work place.

I was surprised that he had remembered my request, and done this, but more was to follow. He actually took me out on sightseeing expeditions. Some of what I saw was uninteresting, and some incomprehensible—there was one small pyramid with nothing in it but colored bubbles that moved in a slow dance up to the apex and down the sloping sides. What the Master said about it made no sense to me at all. And there were several trips to water-gardens, larger versions of the garden pools, which meant a lot of standing and sitting about while he waded through the seething waters. He invited me to admire their beauty, and I dutifully did so. They were quite hideous.

But he also took me to the place Fritz had spoken of, with the turning globe that was covered with a map, and the walls of bright stars that moved against deep blackness when the Master spoke words, in his own tongue, into a machine. These were star maps, and in one of them he showed me the star from one of whose planets the Masters had set out, long, long ago. I tried as well as I could to memorize its position, though it was hard to see what good that would do.

And one day he took me to the Pyramid of Beauty.

A thing that had puzzled me since first coming into the City was that all the slaves were boys.

Eloise, the daughter of the Comte de la Tour Rouge, had been chosen Queen of the Tournament and had afterward gladly gone, as she told me, to serve the Tripods in their City. I had thought I might meet her here, and it was something I wanted and did not want at the same time. It would have been terrible to see her worn down like all the other slaves, her beauty crushed under the weight and clammy heat of this place. But I found no girls, and Fritz, when I asked him, said he had seen nothing of them, either. But on this afternoon, dragging myself along beside my Master, the sweat pooling under my chin, I saw them.

It was not one pyramid that we were approaching, but a series of pyramids which joined together near their bases—half a dozen smaller peaks clustered about a central one. It lay a long way, two ninths (more than half an hour, that is) from the part in which my Master lived, by carriage. I saw many Masters strolling about, a few with attendant slaves. We went into the first pyramid, and I almost cried out at what lay before me: a garden of earthly flowers, with that brightness of reds and blues, yellows and pinks and whites which I had almost forgotten, surrounded by this perpetual green twilight and seeing only the drab, ugly plants of the garden pools.

I realized that I could not touch them: they were protected, by the glass-like material, from the atmosphere of the City. But it took me longer to realize something else: that despite the appearance of life, there was only death here. I saw this first when I noticed, on the crimson velvet of a rose, the golden bead of a bee. It did not move. And looking further, I saw other bees, butterflies, all kinds of pretty insects, but all still. And the flowers themselves were stiff and lifeless.

It was a pageant, a show by which the Masters could see the real life of the world they had conquered. There was even white light, not green, inside, which made the colors shine with a dazzling intensity. Farther on there was a forest glade, with squirrels on the branches, birds somehow suspended in space, a rippling stream, and on its bank an otter with a fish between its jaws. But all frozen, dead. It was nothing like the world I had known, once the shock of false recognition had worn off, because the world I had known had been a living and moving one.

There were dozens of different tableaux, some of them unfamiliar to me. One showed a dark dripping swamp, not unlike some of the Masters' garden pools, with a couple of strange creatures floating in it that might have been queerly shaped logs, but for their gaping jaws, gleaming with vicious white teeth. Some were being rearranged by Masters with face masks somewhat similar to the ones we slaves wore, and my Master told me that they were all changed in turn. But that merely meant exchanging one dead scene for another.

The Master had a special objective in view, however, and we passed all these on our way to the central pyramid. There, a ramp moved up in a narrowing spiral, with exits to different floors. I toiled up after him. I was, as always, tired after a quarter of an hour's walking, and the ramp was quite steep. We did not go out at the first exit. At the second, he led me through a triangular opening, and said, "Look, boy."

I looked, and the salt sweat on my face was mixed with the saltier flow of tears—tears not just of grief, but of anger, more anger, I think, than I had ever felt before.

The Vicar at Wherton had a room he called his study, and in it he had a cabinet of polished wood, with many thin drawers. I was sent to him once, on an errand, and he pulled the drawers out and showed me what they held. Under glass there were rows and rows of butterflies, pinned down, their gay wings outstretched. I thought of that, as I stared at what was exhibited here. For there were rows of caskets, all transparent, and in each casket lay a girl, dressed in her finery.

The Master said, "These are the female humans who are brought to the City. Your people choose them for their beauty, and they are winnowed out again by those Masters who administer this place. There are discards from time to time as better ones are brought in, but the really beautiful ones will be preserved here forever, to be admired by the Masters. Long after the Plan is completed."

I was too full of hate and bitterness even to pay attention to the cryptic remark about the Plan. If only I had one of those iron eggs we had found in the great-city . . . He repeated, "To be admired by the Masters forever. Is that not a fine thing, boy?"

Choking, I said, "Yes, Master. A fine thing."

"It is some time since I looked at them," the Master said. "This way, boy. There are some fine specimens in this row. At times I doubt the destiny of our race, to spread far out across the galaxy and rule it. But at least we appreciate beauty. We preserve the best of the worlds that we find and colonize."

I said, "Yes, Master."

I have said that I both wanted and did not want to find Eloise in the City. Now, in this hideous place, the wanting and the not wanting were increased a thousandfold. My eyes searched hungrily for something from which they could only turn away, in sickness and revulsion.

"Here they all have red hair," the Master said. "Uncommon in your race. The shades of red are different. Observe that they are arranged from light red to deep. I see that there are two new intermediate shades here since my last visit."

It was not red hair my eyes sought, but black—dark hair which I had seen once only, a fuzz growing through the silvery mesh of the Cap, when I had playfully snatched her turban from her in the little garden between the castle and the river.

"Do you wish to go on, boy, or have you seen enough?"

"I would like to go on, Master."

The Master made a small humming noise, which was a sign that he was pleased. I suppose he was glad to think he was making his slave-friend happy. He led the way, and I followed, and at last I saw her.

She was dressed in the simple dark blue gown, trimmed with white lace, which she had worn at the tournament, when the forest of swords flashed silver in the sun, and all the knights acclaimed her as Queen. Her brown eyes were closed, but the ivory of the small oval face was delicately flushed with rose. But for the casket, very much like a coffin, and the hundreds of others around her, I could have thought she was sleeping.

But her head was bare of both crown and turban. Her hair had grown in the weeks that followed that time in the garden. I looked at her close-cropped curls. They covered, but did not quite conceal the one thing she did wear on her head: the Cap which had brought her, joyfully, to this monstrous resting place.

"Also, a fine specimen," said the Master. "Have you seen enough, yet, boy?"

"Yes, Master," I told him. "I have seen enough."

Nine

I Strike a Desperate Blow

The days and the weeks went by. There was always the green dusk, but sometimes the twilight was less dim, and then one knew that outside it was a fine summer day, the sun scorching in a high blue heaven. What one saw inside the City was a pale disk, only visible when it was near the zenith, a small circle of lighter green. But the heat did not vary, nor the crushing weight of one's body. And day by day the heaviness and the hotness drained strength away. Each night I lay down with greater thankfulness on my hard bed; each morning it was a greater effort to rise.

Matters were not helped by the fact that the Master became more and more obviously attached to me. His fondling of me, occasional at first, became a daily ritual, and I was pressed into doing something of the sort in return. There was a place on his back, above the rear tentacle, which he liked to have rubbed and scratched. He would urge me to do this more vigorously, and direct me to spots a little higher or lower. I wore my fingernails down against his tough abrasive hide, and he still called for more. Finally I found an implement—a thing vaguely like a brush but curiously shaped—which produced the same, or a similar effect. This saved my fingernails, but not the muscles of my right arm, as he continued to prod me to further exertion.

One afternoon while doing this I slipped and, his body turning round at the same time, the implement brushed lightly against the other side of him, between his nose and his mouth. The result was startling. He gave forth a wild howling noise, and a moment later I was flat on my back, smashed to the ground by a reflex action of two of his tentacles. I lay there half-stunned. The tentacles reached for me again, and I was sure that now, at any rate, I was in for another beating. But he lifted me to my feet instead.

His action, it appeared, had been instinctive, and defensive. That spot between the two openings was, he explained, a most sensitive one in the Masters. I must be careful not to touch it. A

Master could be badly hurt by being struck in that place. He hesitated a moment, and then went on: a Master might even be killed by such a blow.

I looked as chastened and penitent as a devoted slave ought to do under such circumstances. I went on with the rubbing and scratching on the original site, and he was soon soothed. The leathery tentacles wound themselves around me, like a loathsomely affectionate octopus. Half an hour later, I was excused to my refuge, and I hurried there and, tired as I was, before lying down made a note of this important new fact in the journal that I was keeping.

I had been doing this for some time. As I learned new things, however trivial, I jotted them down. It was better than relying on memory. I still had no idea how I was to get either the journal or myself out of the City, but it was important to go on collecting information. I was proud of my ingenuity over the journal. One of my Master's favors had been to introduce me to the place where human books were kept, and to allow me to bring some of them back, to read during my rest periods. I had found that a blackish liquid which was used in preparing certain of the Master's foods would serve as ink, and I had made myself a primitive pen to write with. Writing was not easy, but I was able to scrawl notes on the margins of the pages of a book; in perfect freedom from discovery since my Master could not come into the refuge, being unable to breathe human air.

Apart from the journal, I also, of course, continued to tell Fritz of these things when we met, and he passed any information he picked up on to me. The City was taking a heavy toll of him—the City, and his Master in particular. Once I did not see him for several days. I went twice to his Master's pyramid, and questioned other slaves in the communal place. The first time, I drew a blank, but on the second I was told that he had been admitted to the slaves' hospital. I asked where that was, and they told me. It was a long way—too far for me to go just then. I had to wait until my Master's next work time.

The hospital was in a section of a pyramid otherwise devoted to stores. It was larger than any of the communal places I had seen, and had beds in it, but there was little sign of luxury. It had been set up at some time in the past by a Master rather more benevolent than the rest, with the purpose of dealing with those slaves who, while they had collapsed from overwork or similar strains, were not yet so worn out that they needed to go to the Place of Happy Release. A slave had been put in charge of it, and had eventually been allowed to choose an assistant, who became his successor. It had carried on since then, unsupervised and for the most part disregarded by the Masters. When a slave collapsed, he was taken to the hospital if he did not quickly recover on his own account. He stayed there, resting, until either he was better or decided that his Happy Release was due.

There was no need for supervision, of course, since the thing the slaves most desired was to serve the Masters or, if they were no longer capable of serving, to end their lives. I found Fritz in a bed a little way off from the three others who were patients at the time, and asked him what had happened. He had been sent on an errand after a beating, with no chance to freshen up in his refuge, and he had collapsed on the way. I asked him how he was now, and he said better. In fact he looked terrible. He said, "I am going back to the Master tomorrow. If he has taken another slave, then I go to the Choosing Place, to see if another Master wants me. But I do not think any will. There is a new batch due shortly, from Games they hold in the east. They will not want one as feeble as I am."

I said, "Then you will go into the general pool of slaves? It may be better."

"No." He shook his head. "Only the new ones who are unclaimed do that."

"Then . . ."

"The Place of Happy Release."

I said, horrified, "They can't make you do it!"

"It would seem strange if I did not want to, and we must do nothing that seems strange." He managed a poor sort of smile. "I don't think it will happen. The new ones have not yet arrived, so my Master will wait also. He will take me back for a while at least, I think. But I must not stay here longer than is necessary."

I said, "We must do more about finding a way out of the City. Then, if something like that did happen to one of us, he could escape."

Fritz nodded. "I have thought of that. But it is not easy."

"If we could get into the Hall of the Tripods, and steal one . . . We might be able to find out how to work the mechanism that drives it."

"I do not think there would be much chance. They are twice as tall as we, remember, and all the things they use in the City—except those like the carriages which are designed for us to work—are out of our reach. And I do not see how we could get into the Hall of the Tripods. We would have to go through the Entering Place, and we would have no excuse for being there."

"There must be *some* way of escaping."

Fritz said, "Yes. We have learned many things that Julius would like to know. One of us must get back to the White Mountains."

On my way back from the hospital, and later, I thought about Fritz. If his Master had taken another slave, after all, and refused to have him back . . . Even if not, he was so weak, and grow-ing weaker. It was not just the beatings: his Master gave him tasks that were, deliberately, beyond his strength. I tried to remember the time, not so long before, when I had resented him for usurping Henry's place on our expedi-tion. Now, although we saw each other only at intervals and for brief periods, I felt closer to him than I had ever done to Henry or Beanpole—as though we were brothers.

One enjoys friendship most when times are good, when the sun shines and the world is kind. But it is the sharing of adversity that knits men together. We were both slaves of these monsters, and of all the slaves in the City, only we two understood what was being done to us: that they *were* monsters we were forced to serve, not gods whom it was a joy to wait on. The misery of this was a bond uniting us. I lay awake a long time that night, worrying about him and trying to plan some way of escape from the City. It was he, plainly, who would need this first. All sorts of crazy notions flitted through my head—such as scaling the inside of the golden wall and cutting a hole through the glass-like stuff which formed the dome. I lay and sweated and despaired.

The next day, I saw Fritz again. He had left the hospital, and his Master had taken him back. He had beaten him again already. The urgency of discovering a way out had retreated, but not far.

I had wondered at one time why the Masters had taken the trouble to learn our languages rather than make the slaves learn theirs, but it was obvious really. The Masters lived far, far longer than normal men, and the slaves in the City were mayflies by comparison. A slave would be worn out by the time he could understand enough to be useful. There were other factors, too, I imagine. By this means, the Masters retained a privacy of expression among themselves. It was also true that they had a way of learning which men did not: they did not need books but somehow passed knowledge from mind to mind, and so it was easier for them to acquire skills of this kind. My Master spoke German to me, but to other slaves from other lands he could speak in their language. It was a thing which amused him: the division of men into different races who could not understand each other. The Masters had always been of one race, it seemed, solitary in themselves but yet part of a unity which men, even before they came, had shown small signs of achieving.

Like other human things, apart from amusing him it also in a way attracted him. He had studied mankind more closely than most of the other Masters—he read the old books, and he still plied me with questions—and his attitude toward us was a strange one. It combined contempt and disgust, fascination and regret. This last came to the fore when he was in one of his moods of melancholy—minor phases of the Sickness—and stayed for long periods in the garden pool, inhaling gas bubbles. It was during one of these that he told me something more about the Plan.

I had taken him a third gas bubble, and been forced to submit to the usual caressing from tentacles slimy from the pool, and he started bemoaning the fact that this wonderful friendship we had could only last so short a time— since I, his dog, destined anyway for a brief human life, must have it curtailed still further by the conditions under which I lived in the City. (It did not occur to him that the curtailing might be prevented by having me released to a normal life outside, and I could not, of course, suggest it without letting it appear that I preferred such a thing to a year or two of glorious misery as his slave.) This was not a new topic. He had dwelt on it before, and I had done my best to look puzzled and adoring and ineffably contented with my lot.

On this occasion, though, the professed unhappiness about my approaching death turned into a form of speculation, and even doubt. It began on a personal level. He had asked me again about my life before I came to the City, and I painted for him the picture, a combination of truth and falsehood, which I had outlined before. (I am sure that sometimes there were inconsistencies, but he did not appear to notice them.) I talked of children's games we had played, and then of the Christmas Feast, which I knew was roughly the same in the south as it had been at Wherton except that, in the mountains, there was more likelihood of snow. I told him of the exchanging of gifts, the service in the church, and the feast after—the roast turkey stuffed with chestnuts and surrounded by glistening brown sausages and golden potatoes, the flaming plum pudding. I described it with some poignancy, because my mouth, despite the heat and my growing weakness, watered at the thought, contrasted with the dreadful food which kept us alive here.

The Master said, "One cannot share another creature's pleasure, especially a lower creature's, but I can tell that this was a joy to you. And if you had not won at the Games, you would have gone on having such joys through many years. Do you ever think of this, boy?"

I said, "But by winning at the Games, I was permitted to come to the City, where I can be with you, Master, and serve you."

He was silent. The brownish mist had finished rising from the gas bubble and, without being bidden, I rose and brought him another.

He accepted it, still silent, put it in place, and pressed it. As the mist rose, he said, "So many of you, year after year—it is a sad thing, boy. But nothing compared with the night-feeling that comes when I think of the Plan. And yet it has to be. This is the purpose of things, after all."

He paused, and I stayed quiet, and eventually he began to talk again. He talked about the Plan.

There were, as I have said, several differences between the world from which the Masters came, and the earth. Their world was bigger, so that things on it weighed much more, and also hotter and wetter. These were things which did not greatly matter. In the City, there were machines which made the heaviness that I knew only too well, but the Masters could have lived without them. The present heaviness was less than had existed on the home planet, and they or their successors could learn to live naturally on a world like this. As for the heat, there were parts of the earth, it seemed, which were hot enough—in the south where the other two Cities were.

But there was, of course, another difference to which they could not adapt themselves: the fact that our atmosphere was as poisonous to them as theirs to us. This meant that outside the enclaves of the Cities they could only be masked; and not just head-masked as we slaves were here, but with their whole bodies covered by a clinging greenish envelope, because the brightness of the sun's light hurt their skins also. In fact, except on extremely rare occasions, outside their Cities they never left the Tripods—in this cold part of the earth, never at all.

All this, though, could be changed, and would be. The success of the expedition, the conquest of this world, had been reported back to the home planet. Samples had been taken—of air, water, other natural constituents. Their wise men had studied them, and in due course the message had been sent: the earth's atmosphere could be altered to enable the Masters to live naturally in it. This colonization would in due course be a complete one.

It would take time. Mighty engines had to be created, and while some parts of them could be made here, others had to be shipped across the gulfs of space. Once they were set up, at a thousand different places on the earth, they would take in our air and breathe out an air suited to the Masters. It would be thick and green, like the air inside the City's dome, and as it spread the sun's light would dim and the living things that now flourished—flowers and trees, animals and birds and men—would choke and die. Within ten years of the setting up of the engines, it was calculated, the planet would be fit for the Masters' habitation. Long before that, the human race would have perished.

I was appalled by what I was told, by the revelation that man's subjugation was not, as we had thought, a final evil, but the precursor of annihilation. I managed to make some inane remark, to the usual effect that whatever the Masters desired was good. My Master said, "You do not understand, boy. But there are some of us who are saddened by the thought that the things and creatures now living on this world must be blotted out. It is a heavy burden to the mind."

I pricked my ears up. Was it possible that the Masters really were divided among themselves, for all that they professed not to understand man's divisions? Was there a possibility of disunity, and could we exploit it? But he went on, "Those of us who feel like this believe that places should be made where some of the creatures could go on living. The Cities, for instance. Things could be arranged so that some men and animals and plants were able to shelter in them. And the Masters could visit them, masked or in sealed carriages, and see these creatures—not dead as they are in the Pyramid of Beauty, but alive. Would this not be a good thing, boy?"

I thought how much I loathed him, loathed all of them, but smiled, and said, "Yes, Master."

"There are some who say this is unnecessary, a waste of resources, but I think they are wrong. After all, we appreciate beauty, we Masters. We preserve the best of the worlds we colonize."

Places where a handful of men and animals could live, under glass, to satisfy the curiosity and vanity of the Masters . . . "We appreciate beauty . . ." There was a silence, in which we thought our different thoughts about what he had just told me. It continued, and the need to know the answer to the one vital question pressed in on me. I had to take the risk of asking him. I said, "When, Master?"

A tentacle moved, in a gesture of interrogation. "When . . . ?" he repeated.

"When will the Plan start, Master?"

He did not reply for a moment, and I thought he might be surprised by my query—suspicious, even. I could read some of his more obvious reactions by this time, but there was a great deal hidden. However, he said, "The great ship is well advanced on its journey back to us, with the things that are needed. In four years, it will be here."

Four short years before the engines began to belch out poison. Julius, I knew, had been assuming that we had time enough—that the next generation, or the one after that, might carry the campaign we had started to a final success. Suddenly time was an enemy, as implacable as the Masters themselves. If we failed and an attempt had to be made next year, we should have lost a quarter of the cruelly short interval in which it was possible to act.

The Master said, "It is a splendid sight when the great ship glides through the night like a shooting star. I hope you will see it, boy."

He meant that he hoped I would live that long: four years represented a very good span for the life of a slave in the City. I said fervently, "I hope so, Master. It will be a glorious and happy moment."

"Yes, boy."

"Can I bring you another gas bubble, Master?"

"No, boy. I think I will eat. You may prepare my table."

Fritz said, "Then one of us must get away."

I nodded. We were in the communal place at Fritz's pyramid. There were half a dozen other slaves present, two of them playing a game of cards, the remainder lying flat and not even talking. It would be the beginning of autumn in the world outside; the air this morning would have a nip in it, perhaps, after an early night frost. In the City the sweltering heat did not change. We sat apart, and talked in low voices.

I said, "You haven't found anything, I suppose?"

"Only that the Hall of the Tripods is impossible. The slaves who work in the Entering Place have nothing to do with those inside the City. They are ones who were not chosen by Masters, and they envy those whom they pass through into the City. They would not let anyone through in the opposite direction."

"If we could trick our way in—attack them . . ."

"There are too many of them, I think. And there is another thing."

"What?"

"Your Master told you about the Tripod being destroyed. They know there is some danger, but they think it is only from un-Capped boys. If they find out we have managed to get into the City, wearing false Caps . . . they ought not to have that warning."

"But if one of us escapes," I argued, "—won't that be enough to warn them, anyway? None of the truly Capped would want to leave the City."

"Except through the Place of Happy Release. There are no checks on who goes there. It must seem as though that is what has happened, and therefore the escape must be secret."

"Any kind of escape is better than none. We have to get this news to Julius and the rest."

Fritz nodded, and I was conscious again of his thinness, his head, although gaunt, large against the frail stalk of his neck. It must be he who escaped, if only one could do so. With a Master kind by their standards, I could hold out for a year or more. He had said he hoped I would see the great ship returning in its glory. But Fritz would not live through this winter unless he got away: that was certain.

Fritz said, "I have thought of one thing."

"What is it?"

He hesitated, and said, "Yes, it is better that you should know, even if it is only an idea. The river."

"The river?"

"It comes into the City, and is purified and made right for the Masters. But it flows out, also. Do you remember that we saw, from the Tripods, the outflow beyond the walls? If we could find the place inside the City . . . there might be a possibility."

"Of course." I thought about it. "It will probably be on the opposite side of the City from where the river flows in."

"Probably, though it need not be. But that is the part where the Masters who do not have slaves live. One cannot search there as easily, for fear of drawing attention to oneself."

"It is worth trying." A number flashed on the wall, and a slave roused himself wearily. "Anything is worth trying."

Fritz said, "As soon as we find a way out, one of us must go."

I nodded. There was no doubt of that, nor of whom the one should be. I thought of the loneliness of staying behind, with no friend in this hideous place, no one to talk to. Except, of course, my Master. That only added a further horror to the prospect. I thought of the autumn world outside, the early snows already falling and lying on the White Mountains, covering the entrance to the Tunnel for another half year. I looked at the clock on the wall, marked in periods and ninths—Masters' time. In a few minutes I would have to put on my mask, and return to take my Master home from his work.

It happened four days later.

I had been sent on an errand by the Master. One of their habits was to rub various oils and ointments into their bodies, and he told me to go to a certain place and get a particular oil. It was something like a shop, with a narrowing spiral ramp in the center and items laid out at different heights. I say a shop, though no one was in charge, as far as I could see, and it seemed that no money was paid. This pyramid to which I was sent was much farther away than the ones I customarily went to. I presumed the oil he wanted—he gave me an empty container to identify it—was not available nearer at hand. I slogged my way across the City, taking well over an hour to get there and back, and returned exhausted and soaked with sweat. I wanted desperately to go to my refuge—to take off the mask and wash and rub myself—but it was unthinkable that a slave should do that without first reporting to his Master. So I went the other way, to the window-room, expecting to find him in the pool. He was not, but in a far corner of the room. I went to him. and made the bow of reverence.

I said, "Do you wish the oil now, Master, or shall I put it with the others?"

He did not answer. I waited a moment or two, and prepared to go away. It might be one of his times of being withdrawn and uncommunicative. Having done my duty, I could put the oil in the cupboard, and go to my refuge until he called me. But as I turned, one of his tentacles snaked out, caught and lifted me. More fondling, I thought, but it was not that. The tentacle held me up, the unwinking eyes surveyed me.

"I knew you were a strange one," said the Master. "But I did not know how strange."

I made no reply. I was uncomfortable but, having grown used to the license he granted me and, to some extent, to the strangeness of his moods, not apprehensive.

He went on, "I wished to help you, boy, because you are my friend. I thought it might be possible to make more comfort for you in your refuge. In one of the storybooks of your people, it tells of a man making for a friend what is called a surprise. This I wished to do. So I sent you away, and put on a mask and went into the refuge. I discovered a curious thing."

It had been held behind him by another tentacle and he produced it and showed it to me: the book in which I had written the notes of what I had learned. I was anxious now, all right. Desperately I racked my mind to think of something to say, some explanation, but nothing came.

"A strange one," he repeated. "One who listens, and writes down in a book. For what purpose? The human who wears a Cap knows that the things concerning the Masters are wonders and mysteries, which it is not good for men to learn. I have talked of them, and you have listened. You were my friend, were you not? Though even so it was odd that you showed little fear of being told that which was forbidden. A strange one, as I said. But to record afterwards, in secret, in your refuge . . . The Cap should forbid that absolutely. Let us examine your Cap, boy."

Now he did what I had feared might happen on the day he beat me, when later he called me back and told me I was to be his friend. While a tentacle held me in mid-air, a second one moved to the lower part of the mask, where the material was soft, and its hard tip probed upwards. I wondered if it would break through the material, so that I choked in the poisonous air, but it did not. I felt the tip, narrowing to needle point but hard and precise, run over the edge of the false Cap I was wearing, probe and pluck.

"Strange, indeed," said the Master. "The Cap is not married to the flesh. Something is wrong here, very wrong. It will be necessary to investigate. You must be examined, boy, by the . . ."

The word he said meant nothing: I suppose he was talking about a special group of Masters who had to do with the Cappings. What was clear was that my situation was desperate. I did not know whether they could read my mind under examination or not, but at least they would know of the existence of the false Caps, and be alerted against our enterprise. They would obviously check all other slaves in the City. In which case, Fritz, too, was lost.

It would be useless to fight against him. Even fully fit, at normal weight, a man was no match for the strength of the Masters. The tentacle had me round the waist, so that my arms were free. But what was the good of that? Unless . . . The central eye, above the creature's nose and mouth, stared at me. He knew something was wrong, but he still did not think of me as a danger. He did not remember what he had told me once, when I was rubbing him and my arm slipped.

I said, "Master, I can show you. Bring me closer."

The tentacle moved me in toward him. I was no more than two feet away. I canted my head to the right, as though to show something concerned with the Cap. The movement hid the start of my next one, until it was too late for him to parry or push me away. Bunching my muscles, I put every ounce of strength I possessed into an upward swinging right hook. It caught him where the implement had brushed him, between nose and mouth, but this time with the full force of my body behind it.

He gave a single howl, which broke off in mid-cry, and at the same time the tentacle holding me hurled me away from him. I hit the floor hard, some yards away, and slid to the very edge of the garden pool. I was barely conscious as I staggered to my feet, and almost fell into the steaming waters.

But the Master had keeled over as he threw me. He lay there, prone and silent.

Ten

Under the Golden Wall

I stood by the pool for a moment, trying to think of what to do. I was dazed from being dashed to the ground, and dazed also by what I had achieved. With much the same blow that had dispatched my opponent in the final at the Games, I had knocked out one of the Masters. Now that I had done it, it seemed incredible. I stared at the great fallen figure with wildly conflicting feelings. Astonishment and pride were mixed with fear; even without being Capped, it was impossible not to feel awe for the power these creatures had, for their size and strength. How had I, a mere human, dared to strike at such a one, even in self-defense?

These feelings faded, though, into a more acute and practical apprehension. What I had done had been unpremeditated, forced on me by the predicament in which I found myself. My situation now was only to a degree less urgent. By striking a Master I had irretrievably shown my hand. I had to decide what action to take next, and decide quickly. He was unconscious, but for how long? And when he recovered . . .

My instinct was to flee, to put myself as far from this place as possible, as quickly as possible. But to do that, I realized, was merely to exchange a small trap for a larger one. I would be tracked down, and easily enough in a place where I could not long survive without going into a refuge or a communal place—where the other slaves, once alerted, would be watching for the fiend who had dared raise a hand against the demi-gods.

I looked across the room. All was still, except for the sparks rising, one by one, in the small transparent pyramid by which the Masters measured time. He had not moved. I remembered again what he had said: a Master could be hurt by being struck in that spot. A Master might even be killed. Was it possible? Surely not. But he had not moved; his tentacles stretched out limp against the floor.

I had to know the truth, which meant examining him. There were places, as with men, where veins ran close to the surface, where, despite the abrasive toughness of their skin, one could feel the slow heavy beat of their blood. I must check for that. But at the thought of approaching him, fear came back, redoubled. Once again I wanted to run for it, to get out of the pyramid at least while the going was good. My legs were trembling. For a moment, I could not move at all. Then I forced myself forward, reluctantly, to where my Master lay.

The tip of one of the tentacles lay nearest to me. I reached down, fearfully, touched it with a shudder, drew back, and then, making a great effort, lifted it. It was slack and fell limply when I dropped it again. I went closer, knelt by the body, and felt for the vein which ran to the base of the tentacle, between it and the central eye. There was nothing, I pressed again and again, overcoming my repulsion. No throb at all.

I stood up and away from him. The incredible was more incredible still. I had killed one of the Masters.

Fritz said, "Are you quite sure of it?"

I nodded. "Positive."

"When they sleep, they look as though they're dead."

"But the pulse still beats. I've noticed it, when he fell asleep once in the garden pool. He's dead, all right."

We were in the communal place at his pyramid. I had sneaked into his Master's home, attracted his attention without the Master seeing me, and whispered that we must meet urgently, and talk. He had come down a ninth later. He had guessed something important had happened, because neither of us had approached the other in this way before. But the truth stunned him, as it had earlier stunned me. Following my assurance that the Master was dead, he was silent.

I said, "I'll have to try to get out somehow. I thought I would try for the Hall of the Tripods, even though the chances are against it. But I thought I'd better tell you first."

"Yes." He braced himself. "The Hall of the Tripods is no good. The best chance is the river."

"But we don't know where the outflow is."

"We can look for it. But we shall need time. When is he likely to be missed?"

"Not until his next duty."

"When is that?"

"Tomorrow. Second period."

It was late afternoon. Fritz said, "That gives us the night. It is the best time for searching, anyway, in a place where slaves are not expected to be. But there is something that must be done first."

"What?"

"They must not discover that someone wearing a Cap is capable of attacking a Master."

"It's a bit late, now that I've done it. I don't see how we could get rid of the body, and even if we did, he's going to be missed."

"It might be possible to make it seem an accident."

"Do you think so?"

"We must try. He told you that being struck in that place might kill, so it has probably happened in the past, perhaps accidentally. I think we must go there at once and see what we can do. There is an errand I have been saving up, which will be my excuse. But better not together. You go, and I will follow in a few minutes."

I nodded. "All right."

I hurried back across the City, but found my steps faltering as I reached the familiar pyramid, and stood outside in the corridor for several seconds, trying to make up my mind to press the button that opened the door. Perhaps I had been wrong. Perhaps there had been a faint pulse which I had not detected and by now he had recovered. Or perhaps he had been found by another of the Masters. It was true their lives were solitary, but they did sometimes visit each other. It could have happened, by ill luck, today. The impulse to run away was strong. I think it was only the realization that Fritz was coming after me that nerved me to the point of going in.

And nothing had changed. He lay there, motionless, silent, dead. I stared at him, once more bemused by the awareness that it had really happened. I was still staring when I heard Fritz's approaching footsteps.

He, too, was awed by the sight, but quickly recovered. He said, "I have an idea which might work. You told me he used the gas bubbles?"

"Yes."

"I have noticed with my Master that he is confused when he has taken many—in his movements as well as his mind. Once he slipped and fell in the garden pool. If it could seem that this had happened with yours . . ."

I said, "He's a long way from the pool."

"We must drag him over there."

I said doubtfully, "Can we? He'll be a tremendous weight."

"We can try."

We dragged him by his tentacles. The touch was hateful, but I forgot that in the effort to move him. At first he seemed rooted to the floor, and I thought we should have to abandon the idea. But Fritz, these days so much weaker than I, was straining his gaunt body to take the load, and it shamed me into pulling harder. He moved a little, then more. Slowly, panting and sweating even more profusely than usual, we dragged him, with many rests, across the room to the pool.

We had to get into the pool ourselves to complete the job. It was very hot, only just bearable, and an unpleasant ooze squelched beneath our feet at the bottom. The water came up to the belt that secured our masks. We waded out, brushing our way through rubbery-like plants, some of which clung to us. We really had to heave now on the tentacles, concerting our pulls and moving the body over the side in sharp jerks. Then suddenly the point of balance was reached, and he half toppled, half slid after us, rolling into the water like a heavy log.

Climbing out, we stared down at him. The Master floated on the steaming water, three quarters submerged, one eye staring sightlessly upward. He took up almost the full width of the pool.

I felt too exhausted to think. I could have dropped to the floor, and lain there. But Fritz said, "The gas bubbles."

We opened half a dozen, pressed them to release the brown murk, and scattered them about the edge of the pool, as the Master would have thrown them after use. Fritz even thought of climbing back into the pool and attaching one of the bubbles to him. Then together we went to the refuge, stripped off our masks, washed and dried ourselves. I needed a rest, and urged Fritz to do the same, but he said he must get back. It was more important than ever to take no unnecessary chances. Night was almost on us; the lemon-green lamps would be lighting up outside. He would return now. When I was ready, I must follow, and wait for him in the communal place at his pyramid. He would come down when his Master was in bed, and together we would go in search of the river.

When he had gone, I lay down for a while, but I was afraid of falling asleep—of waking, perhaps, to find another Master here and the death discovered. So I roused myself and made my preparations. I tore out those pages of the book on which I had scrawled notes, placed them in an empty container, and disposed of the rest of the book in the cupboard which destroyed waste. I stoppered the container and put it inside the mask before I strapped it on.

A thought struck me, and I took two more small containers and left the refuge. I filled one with water from the pool, allowed the other to fill with the Masters' air, and sealed them both. Then I returned to the refuge and put these, too, inside the mask where they rested against my collarbone. Julius might find them useful.

That was, of course, providing we got out of the City. I tried not to think of the odds against it.

I had to wait a long time for Fritz and when he did come I saw that his back and arms were newly marked with welts. He said yes, he had been beaten for being late on the errand. He looked tired and ill. I suggested that he stay behind and rest while I searched for the river on my own, but he would not hear of it. I was hopeless at finding my way in the City and would only wander around in circles. This was quite true: I had only slowly learned to trace a path through the maze, and then just to certain familiar spots.

He said, "Have you eaten lately, Will?"

I shook my head. "I wasn't hungry."

"But you must eat, all the same. I have brought food down. Drink as much as possible, too, and take a salt stick. Change the sponges in your mask before we go out. We do not know how long it will be before we can breathe good air again."

This was true also, and I had thought of none of it. We were alone in the communal place. I swallowed the food he gave me, crumbled a salt stick and ate it, drank water until I thought I was likely to burst. Then I changed the sponges in the mask and strapped it on. I said, "I suppose there's no point in wasting time."

"No." His voice was muffled by his own mask. "We had better start right away."

Outside it was dark, except where the lamps cast small circles of sallow luminescence; I thought they looked like gigantic glow-worms. The heat had not abated, of course. It never did. Almost at once sweat began forming inside my mask. We walked on, with the rolling lurching gait that slaves developed as the best way of coping with the heaviness in their limbs. It was a long way to the sector where Fritz thought the river might make its exit. One of the carriages would have taken us there quite quickly, but it was unthinkable for slaves to travel in a carriage unless a Master were with them. We had to make it on our own plodding feet.

There were few Masters about, and we saw no slaves. On Fritz's suggestion we split up, with him traveling ahead of me, just within range of visibility. One slave out at night could be explained as being on an errand for a still active Master—two together would seem odd. I saw the point in this, though I regretted the separation, and was hard put to keep him in sight while staying the necessary distance apart. We moved from one circle of light to the next, and there was a stage between where one walked through near blackness, with no more than a dim green glow ahead. It was a strain on eye and mind alike, particularly in the follow-my-leader role.

One detected the approach of a Master some way off. Their three round splayed feet made a distinctive flat slapping sound on the smooth hardness of the road. I heard this behind me as I passed under a lamp. It grew louder, since they moved faster than we did. I thought it might come abreast of me in the dark patch, and wanted to dodge away. But there was no side turning here, and anyway it might look suspicious. There was the possibility of losing touch with Fritz, as well. I walked on, remembering a few lines of poetry I had found in an old book at home:

> *Like one that on a lonesome road*
> *Doth walk in fear and dread,*
> *And having once turned round walks on,*
> *And turns no more his head;*
> *Because he knows a frightful fiend*
> *Doth close behind him tread.*

I had not turned around, but then I did not need to, knowing very well what it was that followed. We were in a part of the City entirely strange to me, and I suddenly realized that if I were questioned I had no sort of answer to give. I tried to think of one, but my brain had gone blank.

The dark patch came, and the sounds were still behind me. He should have been up with me by now, I thought, and had a dreadful conviction that he had slowed his progress deliberately, that he was examining me and preparing to accost me. I went on, expecting every moment that the Master's voice would boom out from behind, a tentacle grasp me and swing me off the ground. I could see Fritz's figure dimly, fading into the darkness past the next light. I felt horribly alone, the more so because of the follower, whose slapping footsteps now were right behind me. I wanted to run, but somehow kept to my resolution. And then the huge grotesque shape shambled past me, and I felt like collapsing in the weakness of relief.

But it was not yet over. Fritz had vanished into the next patch of darkness, and the Master disappeared in turn. I made my way after them. Light faded, leaving nothing but the distant glow. This brightened again. I could see the globe of the lamp, lifted on its long angular arm. And just beyond it . . .

The Master was there, and so was Fritz. They stood together, the Master towering over Fritz. I heard a distant sound of speech.

I wanted to turn back into the shadows, but that might attract his attention. I had to go forward, whatever happened. And retreat would mean abandoning Fritz. I marched on. If he were in trouble . . . I did not think much of my chances of landing another sucker punch like the one that had killed my own Master. I found myself trembling, with fear and resolution. Then, with a second flush of relief, I saw the Master move on and Fritz, more slowly, follow.

He waited for me in the next shadows. I said, "What was it? What did he want to know?"

Fritz shook his head. "Nothing. He thought he recognized me as the slave of someone he knew. I think he had a message to give. But I was not the one he wanted, so he went on."

I drew a deep breath into the mask. "I thought we were sunk."

"So did I."

I could not see him in the darkness, but I could hear a tremor in his voice. I said:

"Do you want to rest?"

"No. We must press on."

An hour later, we did rest. There was an open place with a large triangular garden pool, to one side of which trees—something like weeping willows only on a massive scale—drooped their branches down to the ground beside the pool, screening us, once we were inside their shelter, from the view of anyone who passed. Though in fact we had seen no one on the streets or ramps for some time now, and there was no sign of a Master in or near the pool. We stretched out, under the ropy fronds that, although there was no wind or breeze in the City, from time to time brushed lightly against us. The ground pulled us down still, but it was bliss not to fight it, to lie flat and motionless. I would have liked to clear the inside of my mask of sweat, but of course that was impossible.

I said, "Have you been in this part of the City before, Fritz?"

"Once only. We are not far from the edge."

"And opposite where the river comes in?"

"Roughly opposite."

"So when we find the Wall, we can start looking for the outflow."

"Yes. We shall have to be more careful from now on. It is late to be on a night errand, and we are reaching the part where the Masters who have no slaves live. We must go more warily."

"They don't seem to travel about at night, either."

"No. That's lucky. But we can't be absolutely sure of it. Do you feel thirsty?"

"A bit. Not too badly."

"I do. It does no good to think about it, though. Since there are no slaves in this part of the City, there will be no communal places." He rose slowly to his feet. "I think we had better get on, Will."

We saw strange things in our search. One of these was a vast pit, a triangle a hundred yards along each side, where, far down, green light gleamed on a seething viscous liquid in which, at intervals, bubbles slowly rose and popped. In another place there was a complicated structure of metal rods and catwalks, looming up into the dark night, pointing, it seemed, to lights that flashed high above our heads. Once, turning a corner ahead of me, Fritz stopped, but beckoned me to come up with him. I did so quietly, and together we stared at the scene. It was a small garden pool, with only a few low-lying plants. In it were two of the Masters, the first we had seen since coming into this sector. They were locked together in what looked like deadly combat, tentacles interlocked, heaving against each other, the water turbulent with their struggling and rolling. We watched for a moment or two and then, making nothing of it, turned silently and went another way.

In due course we reached the Wall. We came down a ramp between two small pyramids, and it was there. It stretched away on either side, golden even in the dim greenish light of the lamps, curving inward slightly as it was lost in the distance. The surface was smooth and hard and unbroken, offering not even a toehold, and upward as well as to the sides it showed no interruption as far as the eye could see. It was discouraging to look at it.

I said, "Do you think we are near where the river ought to be?"

I saw Fritz's thin ribs rise and fall in the lamplight. I was exhausted, but he much more so. He said, "We should be. But the river would be below ground."

"Will there be a way of getting down to it?"

"We must hope there is."

I looked at the featureless wall. "Which way do we go?"

"It doesn't matter. Left. Do you hear anything?"

"What?"

"The sound of water."

I listened intently. "No."

"Nor do I." He shook his head, as though to rouse himself. "Left will do."

Thirst began to attack me soon after. I tried to dismiss the thought, but it came back insistently. We were searching for water, after all. I thought of it, cold, crystal clear, like the streams that ran down below the White Mountains. The picture was a torment, but I could not put it out of my head.

Wherever there was a ramp leading down, we investigated it. We found ourselves in weird labyrinths, some piled high with crates, drums, metal spheres, others packed with machinery that whined and hummed and sometimes sparked. Most of it was untended, but in a few places there were two or three of the Masters doing things at boards covered with little holes and pimples. We were treading warily, and they did not see us. In one great cavern, gas bubbles were being made. They rolled out of the jaws of a machine down a sloping V-shaped channel and dropped into boxes, which, as they were full, closed themselves and were automatically moved away. In another place, even bigger, food was being manufactured, and I recognized it, by the color and shape of the bag, as being a kind of which my Master was especially fond. Had been fond, I corrected myself. The thought provided a twinge of panic. Had the body been found yet?

Were they already looking for his missing slave?

Going back up a ramp to the surface, Fritz said, "I think left was wrong, perhaps. We have come a long way. We must turn back, and try in the other direction."

"Rest first."

"For a few minutes." He sounded discouraged. "We have not much time."

So we plodded back along the way we had come, stopping every now and then to listen for the rushing sound of distant water but hearing only the noise of the machines. We reached the point at which we had come to the Wall, and toiled on. I became aware of a difference and looking up saw the blackness of the night behind us faintly tinged with emerald. The night was coming to an end. Dawn was breaking, and we were no nearer to finding a way out, no nearer to the elusive river.

The day brightened. Thirst overrode hunger, but physical weakness at times seemed greater than either. The green globes winked out. We saw a Master in the distance, out in the street, and hid behind the edge of a garden pool until he had gone. A quarter of an hour later, we had to dodge two more. I said:

"The streets will be swarming with them soon. We shall have to give it up for now, Fritz, and get back to a place where we can take our masks off and eat and drink."

"In a few hours they will find him."

"I know. But what else can we do?"

He shook his head. "I must rest."

He lay down, and I lowered myself to lie beside him. I felt giddy with weakness and thirst tore at my throat like a furious animal. Fritz seemed to be in an even worse state. At any rate, we must not stay here. I told him we ought to get up, and he did not answer. I got to my knees, and pulled his arm. Then he said, his voice suddenly kindled with excitement, "I think . . . Listen."

I listened, and heard nothing. I told him so. He said, "Lie down, and put your ear to the ground. Sound travels better that way. Listen!"

I did and, after a moment, heard it: a thin rushing sound that might be the whisper of distant waters. I pressed my ear closer to the surface of the road, hurting my face against the hardness of the mask. It was there, all right, though far away, a tumultuous torrent. Thirst was sharpened even more by the tantalizing sound, but I felt able to ignore that, too. At last we had found the river. That is to say, we knew approximately where it was. The actual finding could take quite a bit longer.

We systematically tried all the downward ramps in the area, testing them by listening to the ground. Sometimes the noise was louder, sometimes fainter. Once we lost it altogether, and had to cast back on our trail. There were avenues which were deceptively promising but which proved useless, leading to dead ends. More and more often we had to dodge Masters, or lie low till they had passed. One promising ramp led to a huge hall in which a score or more of them did things in front of benches: the river might well be somewhere at the far end, but we dared not go through. And time was passing; above ground we were in full day. Then, quite unexpectedly, we came on it.

A very steep ramp, on which we found ourselves slipping and in danger of falling, led across a level space and dipped again, curving around on itself. Fritz clutched my arm, and pointed. Ahead lay a cavern with an arched roof, in which there were stacks of crates the height of a man. At the far end, only dimly visible in the light of the lemon-green globes which hung at intervals from the ceiling, water gushed from a huge hole and formed a pool, some fifty feet across.

"Do you see?" Fritz asked. "The Wall."

It was true. At the end of the cavern, beyond the pool, there was the dull gleam of gold, unmistakably the inner surface of the barrier which ringed the City, and on which the great dome rested. The pool frothed against it. The water gushing in was that which had circulated through the City, the waste and overflow of hundreds of garden pools. Steam rose up from it. It filled the pool, and from the pool . . . it must go out, under the Wall: there could be no other explanation.

Cautiously we made our way along the cavern, between the stacked crates, to the edge of the pool. There were things like vertical nets in the water, we saw, and we saw also that the water only steamed at its entry point. Nearer to the Wall, Fritz reached down and put a hand in it.

"It is quite cool here. The nets must take the heat out, so it is not lost to the City." He stared down into the churning depths, green from the lamps hanging over them. "Will, let the current take you. Before you go, I will put sealer on the air vents of your mask. There is enough air inside a mask to give you five minutes' breathing: I have tried this out."

What he called "sealer" was a substance the Masters used for closing containers that had been opened. It came out of a tube liquid, but dried and hardened almost right away.

I said, "I'll do yours first."

"But I am not coming."

I stared at him. "Don't be silly. You must."

"No. They must not suspect anything."

"But they'll do that when they find I've gone."

"I do not think so. Your Master died, from a fall, an accident. What would a slave do then? I think he might go to the Place of Happy Release, because there is no point in him going on living."

I saw the force of the argument, but said dubiously, "They might think that, but we can't be sure."

"We can help them to think it. I know some of the slaves in your pyramid. If I tell one that I saw you, and you said that was where you were going . . ."

I saw that, too. Fritz had worked things out very well. I said, "If you escaped, and I went back . . ."

He said patiently, "It would not help, would it? It is your Master that is dead, not mine—you who should go to the Place of Happy Release. If you go back, they will question you. It would be fatal."

"I don't like it," I said.

"It doesn't matter what you like, or I like. One of us must get away, to take the news of what we have learned back to Julius. It is safer if it is you." He squeezed my arm. "I will get out. It is easy now I know where the river is. In three days, I will tell the other slaves in my pyramid that I am too sick to work, and therefore have chosen the Happy Release. I will hide out of the way, and come down here at night."

I said, "I will wait for you outside."

"Wait three days, no longer. You must get back to the White Mountains before winter sets in. And now you must hurry." He forced a smile.

"The sooner you dive, the sooner I can get back, and have a drink of water."

He spread the sealer on the air vents of my mask, after first telling me to take a deep breath. In a few seconds he nodded, indicating the seal was hard. He pressed my arm again, and said, "Good luck." The sound was fainter, more muffled than usual.

I dared delay no longer. The surface of the pool was about six feet below the top of the low containing wall. I climbed up on this and dived down, deep down, into the swirling waters.

Eleven

Two Go Home

Down, down, into darkness. The current tugged me, and I went with it, pulling myself through the water in a crude and feeble attempt at swimming. I swam forward as well as down. My hand touched something and, as my shoulder banged painfully against it, I knew I was at the Wall. But still unbroken, with no sign of an opening, and the current still dragging down.

Possibilities and fears crowded in on me. The water might flow out through gratings, which I would be unable to remove. Or there might be more nets, and I would tangle myself in them. There was a pressure of air in my lungs, the beginning of a roaring in my head. I breathed out a little, and drew a small breath of air in. Five minutes, Fritz had said. How long had I been under already? I realized that I had no idea—it might be ten seconds, or ten times that. Panic, the fear of drowning, clutched me, and I wanted to turn and swim back up, against the pull of water, up to the surface where I had left Fritz.

I swam on and down, trying to blank my mind to everything but the need to hold on. If I abandoned the attempt now, we were lost, anyway. And we must not lose. One of us had to get through. Far above me there was a dim green radiance, but darkness was all around and below me, and I was diving deeper and deeper into it. I took another shallow breath, to ease my aching lungs. I wondered if already I were past the point of no return. Then there was turbulence, the current breaking up and changing direction. I reached forward, and there was still an impassable solidity. Down, down . . . to an edge, an opening. The tide took me into it and I realized that now, finally, I was committed. The current was stronger, more closely channeled. I had to go on, because there was no hope of getting back.

So I swam and was carried along, in utter blackness. I took shallow breaths when I felt I must. Time, as it passed, became more and more immeasurable. There was a sense of having been hours down here, not minutes. Occasionally I bumped my head against the hard surface above me; if I pushed down a foot or two I could touch the bottom. Once my outstretched hand brushed against a side wall. The conduit was about five feet across.

Shallow breaths were no longer enough: I had to inhale more deeply. And this did not help, either. I was breathing in my own exhaled breath. I felt a hammering inside my head. A blackness was growing there, to match the blackness of the water. I was in a trap with no way out. I was finished in fact; and so was Fritz, and those we had left behind in the White Mountains—all mankind. I might as well give up, stop struggling. And yet . . .

It was the faintest of glimmerings at first, something that only inextinguishable optimism could read as light. But I flailed on with weary arms, and it grew. Brightness filtering through— white light, not green. It must be the end of the tunnel. The pain in my chest was savage, but I found I could ignore it. Nearer, brighter, but still out of reach. Another stroke, I told myself, and another, and another. The brightness was right over me, and I kicked and fought my way up to it. Brighter and brighter, and a bursting through to the eye-piercing brilliance of the open sky.

The sky, but not the air for which my tortured lungs were crying out. The sealed mask held me. I tried to release the buckle of the belt, but my fingers were too feeble. I was being carried downriver, the mask buoying me up. Buoying, and also suffocating. I tried again, and failed again. What a terrible irony, I thought, that I should have got so far, only to choke to death in freedom. I clawed at the mask ineffectually. I was filled with a sense of failure, and shame, and anger and then the blackness, for so long barely held at bay, swooped down and swallowed me.

My name first being spoken, but from a long way off.

"Will . . ."

There was something wrong about that, I thought drowsily. It was my name, but . . . pronounced in the English fashion, not with the initial "V" to which I had grown accustomed since we had been speaking German. Was I dead, I wondered? In Heaven, perhaps?

"Are you all right, Will?"

Did they speak English in Heaven? But it was English with an accent—a voice I remembered. Beanpole! Was Beanpole in Heaven, too?

I opened my eyes, and saw him kneeling above me, on the river's muddy bank. He said, with relief, "You *are* all right."

"Yes." I gathered my scattered senses. A bright autumn morning—the river flowing beside us—the sun, from which my unaccustomed eyes automatically turned away—and, farther off . . . There was the great rampart, topped by the vast green crystal bubble. I really was outside the City. I stared at him.

"But how did you get here?"

The explanation was simple. When Fritz and I had gone, taken by the Tripods, he had intended to go back to the White Mountains and tell Julius what had happened. But he had not been eager for it, and had stayed in the town a few days, listening for anything that was said that might be useful. One thing he learned was the approximate site of the City, and he thought he might as well go and take a look at it. It lay, he was told, across a tributary of the great river down which we had come together. He took the hermit's boat, and paddled south and east.

Having found it, he decided to survey it. He dared not risk approaching the Wall by day, but on nights when there was moonlight—some, but not too much—he made his investigations. The result was not encouraging. There was no break in the Wall, and no hope of scaling it. One night he dug down several feet, but the Wall continued still farther, and he had to fill in the hole and leave as dawn broke. None of the Capped approached the City, so he was safe from their attentions. There were farms within reach, and he lived on what food he could pick up or steal.

Once he had been right around the City, there seemed little point in staying on. But it was then that the thought occurred to him, too, that if anyone were going to escape, the river provided what was probably the only route. Its waters, plainly, were waste from the City—nothing grew on the banks for a mile downstream, there were no fish, though plenty in the stretch of river above the City, and he found strange items of debris from time to time. He showed me some— various empty containers, including a couple of empty gas bubbles, which ought to have gone into one of the waste-disposal cupboards but had found their way into the river instead. One after- noon, he saw something quite large floating in midstream. It was too far for him to see clearly, particularly since his eyes, without his lenses, were weak, but he took the boat out and salvaged it. It was of metal, hollow so that it floated, meas- uring some six feet by two, and a foot thick. If that could come out of the City, he argued, a man could. Because of that, he resolved to take up a position where he could watch the outflow— watch, and wait.

And so he had stayed there, while the days and the weeks went by. As time passed, his hopes that one of us might get away dwindled. He had no notion of what things were like inside the City: we might have been discovered to be falsely Capped on the first day, and killed. He stayed on, more, he said, because leaving would mean aban- doning the last shred of hope than because hope had anything to feed on. Now, with the autumn, he realized that he could not delay much longer if he were to get back to the White Mountains before the heavy snows. He had decided to give it another week, and on the morning of the fifth day had seen something else floating down river. He had taken the boat out again, found me, and with a knife ripped open the soft part of the mask to let me breathe.

He said, "And Fritz?"

I told him, briefly. He was silent, and then said, "What do you think the chances are?"

I said, "Not good, I'm afraid. Even if he finds his way back to the river, he's much weaker than I am."

"He said he would try in three days?"

"Yes, three days."

"We'll keep a close watch. And your eyes are better than mine."

We gave him three days, and three times three days, and three days beyond that, each time finding a less convincing argument for our vigil. Nothing came out of the City, that we could see, except ordinary debris. On the twelfth day, there was a snowstorm, and we huddled, shivering, cold and hungry, under the upturned boat. The next morning, without discussion, we set out under a watery sun peering through gray clouds, toward the great river and the south.

Once I looked back. Alongside the river the snow was melting, but the land still stretched bare and white on either side. The river was a gray arrow in an alabaster desert, pointing to the circle of gold and the dome of green crystal. I lifted my arm; it was still a positive joy to be free of the leaden weight which had crushed me for so long. Then I thought of Fritz, and the joy was turned to sadness, and a deep and bitter hatred against the Masters.

We were going home, but only to arm ourselves and others. We would come back.

Don't miss the next book
in the Tripods series:

THE POOL
OF FIRE

Here's a peek!

A Plan of Action

Everywhere there was the sound of water. In places it was no more than a faint whisper, heard only because of the great stillness all around; in others, an eerie distant rumbling, like the voice of a giant talking to himself in the bowels of the earth. But there were places also where its rushing was clear and loud, and the actual torrent was visible by the light of oil lamps, flinging itself down dark rocky water-courses or spilling in a fall over a sheer edge of stone. And places where the water lay calm in long black reaches, its sound muted to a monotonous drip . . . drip . . . drip . . . which had continued for centuries and would continue for as many more.

I was relieved from guard to go to the conference, and so went through the dimly lit tunnels late and alone. The work of nature here mingled with the work of man. The earth's convulsions, and the action of long-dead rivers, had hollowed out these caverns and channels in the limestone hills, but there were marks of the ancients, too. Men had been here in the past, smoothing uneven floors, widening narrow gaps, sinking handrails into an artificial stone to aid and guide the traveler. There were also long ropelike cables, which had once carried the power called electricity to light bulbs of glass along the way. Our wise men, Beanpole had told me, had learned the means of doing this again, but needed resources that were not available to them here—nor would be, perhaps, while men were forced to skulk like rats in the dark corners of a world governed by the Tripods, those huge metal monsters who strode on three giant legs across the face of the earth.

I have told already how I left my native village, at the urging of a strange man who called himself Ozymandias. This happened during the summer which was to have been my last before I was presented for the Capping ceremony. In that, boys and girls in their fourteenth year were taken up into one of the Tripods and returned later wearing Caps—a metal mesh that fitted close to the skull and made the wearer utterly obedient to our alien rulers. There were always a few whose minds broke under the strain of Capping, and these became Vagrants, men who could not think properly and who wandered aimlessly from place to place. Ozymandias had posed as one of them. In fact, his mission was to recruit people who would fight against the Tripods.

So I went, with my cousin Henry who also lived in my village, and later with Beanpole, a long journey to the south. (His real name was Jean-Paul, but we nicknamed him Beanpole because he was so tall and thin.) We arrived at last at the White Mountains, where we found the colony of free men Ozymandias had spoken of. From there, the following year, three of us were sent as a spearhead to penetrate into the City from which the Tripods came and learn what we could of them. Not quite the same three, however. Henry was left behind, and in his place we had Fritz, a native of the land of the Germans in which the City stood. He and I had got into the City, served as slaves of the Masters—monstrous three-legged, three-eyed reptilian creatures who came from a distant star—and learned something of their nature and their plans. But only I had escaped, plunging through the drain of the City into a river, and from there being rescued by Beanpole. We had waited, hoping Fritz might do the same, until, with snow falling and winter coming on, we had been forced to return, heavy-hearted, to the White Mountains.

We had reached them to find that the colony had moved. This had been the result of a prudent decision by Julius, our leader. He had foreseen the possibility of our being unmasked by the enemy, and of our minds being ransacked once we were helpless in their grasp. So, without telling us of it, the plan had been formed to evacuate the Tunnel in the White Mountains, leaving only a few scouts to await our hoped-for return. The scouts had discovered Beanpole and myself, as we stared miserably around the deserted fortress, and had led us to the new headquarters.

This lay a long way to the east, in hilly rather than mountainous country. It was a land of narrow valleys, flanked by barren, mostly pine-wooded hills. The Capped kept to the valley floors, we to the ridges. We lived in a series of caves that ran, tortuously, for miles through the heights. Fortunately there were several entrances. We had guards on them all, and a plan for evacuation in case of attack. But so far all had been quiet. We raided the Capped for food, but were careful to have our raiding parties travel a long way from home before they pounced.

Now Julius had called a conference and I, as the only person who had seen the inside of the City—seen a Master face to face—was summoned from guard duty to attend it.

•••

In the cave where the conference was held, the roof arched up into a darkness that our weak lamps could not penetrate: we sat beneath a cone of night in which no star would ever shine. Lamps flickered from the walls, and there were more on the table, behind which Julius sat with his advisers on roughly carved wooden stools. He rose to greet me as I approached, although any physical action caused him discomfort, if not pain. He had been crippled in a fall as a child, and was an old man now, white-haired, but red-cheeked from the long years he had spent in the thin bright air of the White Mountains.

"Come and sit by me, Will," he said. "We are just starting." It was a month since Beanpole and I had come here. At the outset I had told all I knew to Julius and others of the Council and handed over the things—samples of the Masters' poisonous green air, and water from the City—which I had managed to bring with me. I had expected some kind of swift action, though I did not know what. Swift, I thought, it had to be. One thing I had been able to tell them was that a great ship was on its way, across space, from the home world of the Masters, carrying machines that would turn our earth's atmosphere into air which they could breathe naturally, so that they would not have to stay inside the protective domes of the Cities. Men, and all other creatures native to the planet, would perish as the choking green fog thickened. In four years, my own Master had said, it would arrive, and the machines would be set up. There was so little time.

Julius might have been speaking to me, answering my doubts. He said, "Many of you are impatient, I know. It is right that you should be. We all know how tremendous a task we face, and its urgency. There can be no excuse for action unnecessarily delayed, time wasted. Every day, hour, minute counts.

"But something else counts as much or more; and that is forethought. It is *because* events press so hard on us that we must think and think again before we act. We cannot afford many false moves—perhaps we cannot afford any. Therefore your Council has deliberated long and anxiously before coming to you with its plans. I will give you them in broad detail now, but each one of you has an individual part to play, and that will be told you later."

He stopped, and I saw that someone in the semicircle in front of the table had risen to his feet. Julius said, "Do you wish to speak, Pierre? There will be opportunity later, you know."

Pierre had been on the Council when we first came to the White Mountains. He was a dark, difficult man. Few men opposed Julius, but he had done so. He had, I had learned, been against the expedition to the City of Gold and Lead, and against the decision to move from the White Mountains. In the end, he had left the Council, or been expelled from it; it was difficult to be sure which. He came from the south of France, from the mountains which border on Spanish land. He said, "What I have to say, Julius, is better said first than last."

Julius nodded. "Say it, then."

"You talk of the Council coming to us with its plans. You talk of parts to play, of men being told what they must do. I would remind you, Julius; it is not Capped men you are talking to, but free. You should rather come to us asking than ordering. It is not only you and your Councillors who can plan how to defeat the Tripods. There are others who are not lacking in wisdom. All free men are equal, and must be given the rights of equality. Common sense as well as justice demands this."

He stopped speaking, but remained on his feet, among the more than a hundred who squatted on the bare rock. Outside it was winter, with even these hills mantled with snow, but, as in the Tunnel, we were protected by our thick blanket of rock. The temperature never changed here, from one day or season to another. Nothing changed here.

Julius paused for a moment, before he said, "Free men may govern themselves in different ways. Living and working together, they must surrender some part of their freedom. The difference between us and the Capped is that we surrender it voluntarily, gladly, to the common cause, while their minds are enslaved to alien creatures who treat them as cattle. There is another difference, also. It is that, with free men, what is yielded is yielded for a time only. It is done by consent, not by force or trickery. And consent is something that can always be withdrawn."

Pierre said, "You talk of consent, Julius, but where does your authority lie? In the Council. And who appoints the Council? The Council itself does, under your control. Where is the freedom there?"

"There will be a time," Julius said, "for us to discuss among ourselves how we shall be governed. That day will come when we have destroyed those who now govern humanity all over the world. Until then, we have no room for squabbling or dispute."

Pierre began to say something, but Julius raised a hand and silenced him.

"Nor do we have room for dissension, or the suspicion of dissension. Perhaps what you have said was worth saying, whatever the motive with which you said it. Consent, among free men, is given and can be withdrawn. It can also be affirmed. So I ask: will any man who wishes to challenge the authority of the Council, and its right to speak for this community, rise to his feet?"

He stopped. There was silence in the cave, apart from the shuffle of a foot and the unending distant roar of water. We waited and watched for a second man to get to his feet. None did. When time enough had gone by, Julius said, "You lack support, Pierre."

"Today. But perhaps not tomorrow."

Julius nodded. "You do well to remind me. So I will ask for something else. I ask you now to approve this Council as your government until such a time as those who call themselves the Masters are utterly defeated." He paused. "Will those in favor stand up?"

This time, all stood. Another man, an Italian called Marco, said, "I vote the expulsion of Pierre, for opposing the will of the community."

Julius shook his head. "No. No expulsions. We need every man we have, every man we can get. Pierre will do his part loyally—I know that. Listen. I will tell you what we plan. But first I would like Will here to talk to you of what it is like inside the City of our enemies. Speak, Will."

When I had told my story to the Council, I had been asked by them to keep silent to others for the time being. Normally this would not have been easy. I am talkative by nature, and my head was full of the wonders I had seen inside the City—the wonders, and the horrors. My mood, though, had not been normal. On the way back, with Beanpole, my energies had been taken up by the arduousness and uncertainty of the journey: there had been little time in which to brood. But after we had come to the caves it had been different. In this world of perpetual lamp-lit night, of echoing silences, I could think and remember, and feel remorse. I found I had no wish to talk to others of what I had seen, and what had happened.

Now, under Julius's instruction to speak, I found myself in confusion. I spoke awkwardly, with many stops and repetitions, at times almost incoherently. But gradually, as I continued with my story, I became aware of how closely they were all listening to it. As I went on, also, I was carried away by my recollection of that terrible time—of what it had been like to struggle under the intolerable burden of the Masters' heavier gravity, sweating in the unvarying heat and humidity, watching fellow slaves weaken and collapse under the strain, and knowing this would almost certainly be my own fate in the end. As it had been Fritz's. I spoke, Beanpole told me later, with passion and with a fluency that was not naturally mine. When I had finished and sat down, there was a silence in my audience that told how deeply the story had affected them.

Then Julius spoke again.

"I wanted you to listen to Will for several

reasons. One is that what he says is the report of someone who has actually witnessed the things of which he tells. You have heard him, and you know what I mean: what he has described to you he has seen. Another reason is to hearten you. The Masters are possessed of tremendous power and strength. They have traveled the unimaginable distances that lie between the stars. Their lives are so long that ours, by comparison, seem like the dance of mayflies for a brief day over a tumbling river. And yet . . ."

He paused, and looked at me with a little smile.

"And yet Will, an ordinary boy, no brighter than most, a trifle on the small side—Will has struck at one of these monsters, and seen it collapse and die. He was lucky, of course. There is a place where they are vulnerable to a blow, and he was fortunate enough to discover it and to strike there. The fact remains that he killed one of them. They are not all-powerful. We can take heart from that. What Will managed by luck, we can achieve by planning and resolution.

"This leads me to my third point, my third reason for wanting you to hear Will's story. It is that essentially it is a story of failure." He was looking at me, and I felt myself flushing. He went on, calmly and unhurriedly: "The Master was made suspicious by finding in Will's room the notes he had made about the City and its dwellers. Will did not think the Master would go into his room, where he would have to wear a mask to be able to breathe; but this was shallow thinking. After all, he knew his Master was one who took more care of his slaves than most, and knew that he had, before his own time, arranged for small extra comforts to be installed in the refuge room. It was reasonable that he might do so again, and find the book with notes in it."

His tone was level, considering rather than critical, but the more damning for that. My shame and embarrassment grew as I listened to him.

"Will was able, with Fritz's help, to salvage a great deal from the situation. He escaped from the City, and returned with information whose value to us is beyond computing. But still more could have been gained." His eyes were on me again. "And with time to plan things better, Fritz might have come back, too. He passed on to Will as much as he could of what he had learned, but it would have been better if he had been able to testify himself. Because every tiny item counts in the struggle."

Julius spoke then of the short time we had, of the ship already on its way toward us through the far deeps of space, and of the final death for all earthly things which it would bring with it. And he told us what had been decided by the Council.

The most important thing was to speed up—tenfold, a hundredfold, eventually a thousandfold—our efforts to win the young, those still not Capped, to our side. To do this, as many as possible must go out, winning over and teaching young people, all over the world. Cells of resistance must be set up, and must create other cells. The Council had maps, and would give instructions where to go. Particularly, we must aim at establishing opposition groups in the neighborhood of the other two Cities of the Masters—one thousands of miles across land to the east, the other on the far side of the great ocean to the west. There were problems of languages which would have to be overcome. There were other problems—of survival, of organization—which might seem, at first sight, insuperable. They were not insuperable, because they must not be. There could be no weakening, no despair, nothing but a determination to give every last ounce of energy and strength to the cause.

This course, obviously, involved a risk of alerting the Masters to the opposition that was developing. It was possible that they would not bother much about it, since their plan for extermination was so far advanced. But we had to be prepared for countermeasures. We must not have one headquarters, but a dozen, a hundred, each capable of carrying on by itself. The

Council would split up, its members traveling from place to place, only meeting occasionally and with due precaution.

So much for the first part of the Plan—the urgent need to mobilize all available forces for the struggle, and to reconnoiter and establish colonies within reach of all three enemy Cities. There was another part, perhaps even more important. Means had to be devised for destroying them, and this would involve much hard work and experimentation. A separate base was to be set up, but only those allotted to it would know where it was. That was where our ultimate hope lay. We dare not risk its discovery by the Masters.

"Now," Julius said, "I have told you what I can. Later, you will be given your individual instructions, and the things, such as maps, which you may need to carry them out. I will ask now: are there any questions, or suggestions?"

No one spoke, not even Pierre. Julius said:

"Then we can go our ways." He paused. "This is the last time we shall meet together, in such an assembly, until our task is completed. The only final thing I would say is what I have said already. That which we have to do is a tremendous and frightening task, but we must not let it frighten us. It can be done. Yet it can only be done by each one giving his all. Go now, and God go with you."

●●●

It was Julius himself who gave me my instructions. I was to travel to the south and east, posing as a trader with a packhorse, winning recruits and seeding resistance, and reporting back to the center.

Julius asked, "Is it clear to you, Will?"

"Yes, sir."

"Look at me, Will."

I raised my eyes. He said, "I think you are still smarting, lad, from some of the things I said, after you had told your tale to the assembly."

"I realize that what you said was true, sir."

"But that does not make it easier to bear, when one has told a story of courage and skill and high endeavor, and finds it afterward painted a somewhat different color."

I did not answer.

"Listen, Will. What I did, I did for a purpose. The standards we set ourselves must be high, to a point of near impossibility. So I used your story to point a moral: that carelessness, in one man, can destroy us—that enough is never enough—that there can be no complacency, however much is achieved, because there is always more to achieve. But I can tell you now that what you did, you and Fritz, was of tremendous value to us all."

I said, "Fritz did more. And Fritz did not come back."

Julius nodded. "It is a thing you have to suffer. But what matters is that one of you came back—that we did not lose a year out of the brief time we have. We all have to learn to live with our losses, and to use our regrets to spur us on in the future." He put a hand on my shoulder. "It is because I know you that I can say you did well. You will remember it, but you will remember my criticism more clearly and for longer. Isn't that true, Will?"

"Yes, sir," I said. "I think it is true."

The three of us—Henry, Beanpole, and I—met at a place we had found where there was a fissure high up in the rock, through which a little weak daylight filtered—just about enough for us to make out each other's faces without the need of lamps. It was some distance from those parts of the caves which were in general use, but we liked going there because of the reminder that the world outside, normally only glimpsed during guard duty at one of the entrances, really did exist: that somewhere there was light and wind and weather, in place of this static blackness and the rumble and whisper and drip of underground water. One day, when there must have been a violent storm blowing outside, a fine mist of rain was driven through the crack and filtered down into our cave. We turned our faces up to it, relishing the cool dampness, and imagining we could smell trees and grass in it.

Henry said, "I'm to go across the western ocean. Captain Curtis is taking us, in the *Orion*. He will pay off his crew in England except for the one who is false-Capped like himself, and those two will sail her down to a port in the west of France, where we shall join them. Six of us. The land we are going to is called America, and the people there speak the English tongue. What about you, Will?"

I told them briefly. Henry nodded, clearly thinking his own the better and more interesting mission. I agreed with him in that; but I did not care much either.

Henry said, "And you, Beanpole?"

"I don't know where."

"But they've allocated you, surely?"

He nodded. "To the research base."

It was what one should have expected. Beanpole, obviously, was the sort they would need to work things out for the attack against the Masters. The original trio, I thought, really would be split up this time. It did not seem to matter a great deal. My mind was on Fritz. Julius had been quite right: it was what he had said in criticism that I remembered and, remembering, was shamed by. With another week or so to prepare, we might both have escaped. It was my carelessness that had precipitated matters and led to Fritz being trapped. It was a bitter thought, but inescapable.

The other two were talking, and I was content to let them. They noticed this in time. Henry said:

"You're very quiet, Will. Anything wrong?"

"No."

He persisted. "You've been quiet altogether lately."

Beanpole said, "I read a book once about those Americans to whose land you will be going, Henry. It seems that they have red skins, and go about dressed in feathers, and they carry things like hatchets, and play on drums when they go to war and smoke pipes when they want to be peaceful."

Beanpole was usually too much interested in objects—in the way they worked or could be made to work—to pay any great attention to people. But I realized that he had noticed my unhappiness and guessed the cause of it—after all, he had shared with me the vain wait outside the City, and the journey home—and was doing what he could to distract Henry from questioning and me from brooding. I was grateful for that, and for the nonsense he was talking.

There were many things to do before I could set off. I was instructed in the ways of a packman, taught something of the language in the countries I would visit, advised on how to set up resistance cells and what to tell them when I moved on. All this I took in conscientiously, and with a determination to make no mistakes this time. But the melancholy I felt did not lift.

Henry left before I did. He went in high spirits, in a party that included Tonio, who had been my sparring partner and rival before we went north to the Games. They were all very cheerful. It seemed that everyone in the caves was, apart from me. Beanpole tried to cheer me up, but without success. Then Julius called me to see him. He gave me a lecture on the futility of self-recrimination, the importance of realizing that the only good lesson to be learned from the past was how to avoid similar errors in the future. I listened, and agreed politely, but the black mood did not lift. He said then:

"Will, you are taking this the wrong way. You are someone who does not easily bear criticism, and perhaps least of all from yourself. But to settle into such a mood is something that makes you less capable of doing what the Council requires of you."

"The job will be done, sir," I said. "And properly this time. I promise that."

He shook his head. "I am not sure that such a promise will serve. It would be different if you were of Fritz's temper. Yes, I will speak of him, even though it hurts you. Fritz was melancholic by nature, and could tolerate his own gloom. I do not think this is so with you, who are sanguine and impatient. In your case, remorse and despondency could be crippling."

"I shall do the best I can."

"I know. But will your best be enough?" He looked at me, in slow scrutiny. "You were to have started your journey in three days' time. I think we must delay it."

"But, sir . . ."

"No buts, Will. It is my decision."

I said, "I am ready now, sir. And we do not have the time to waste."

Julius smiled. "There was something of defiance there, so all is not lost. But you are already forgetting what I said at the last assembly. We cannot afford false moves, or plans or people who are not fully prepared. You will stay here a while longer, lad."

I think I hated Julius in that moment. Even when I had got over that, I was bitterly resentful. I watched others leave, and chafed at my own inactivity. The dark sunless days dragged by. I knew that I must change my attitude, but could not. I tried, attempting to put on a false cheerfulness but knew no one, Julius least of all, was deceived. At last, though, Julius called me back.

He said, "I have been thinking about you, Will. I believe I have found an answer."

"May I go, sir?"

"Wait, wait! As you know, some packmen

travel in pairs, for company and so as to protect their goods better from thieves. It might be a good idea for you to have such a companion."

He was smiling. Angry again, I said, "I am well enough by myself, sir."

"But if it is a question of going with another, or staying here—which will you choose?"

It was galling to think that he regarded me as unfit to be sent out on my own. But there was only one answer that it was possible to give. I said, not without sulkiness, "Whatever you decide, sir."

"That's good, Will. The one who is to go with you . . . would you like to meet him now?"

I could see his smile in the lamplight. I said stiffly, "I suppose so, sir."

"In that case . . ." His eyes went to the dark shadows at the edge of the cave, where a row of limestone pillars made a curtain of stone. He called:

"You can come forward."

A figure approached. I stared, thinking that the dimness of the light must be deceiving me. It was easier to disbelieve my eyes than to accept that someone had come back from the dead.

For it was Fritz.

He told me later all that had happened. When he had seen me plunge into the river that led out of the City, under the Golden Wall, he had returned and covered my traces as he had said he would, spreading the story that I had found my Master floating in his pool and had gone right away to the Place of Happy Release, not wishing to live once my Master was dead. It was accepted, and he was ready to make the attempt to follow me out. But the hardships he had suffered, together with the extra exertions of the night we had spent searching for the river, had taken their toll. He collapsed a second time, and a second time was taken to the slaves' hospital.

It had been agreed that, if I got out, I should wait three days for him to follow. More than that time had passed before he was fit even to rise from his bed, and he thought therefore that I would have gone on. (In fact, Beanpole and I waited twelve days before despair and the coming of the snow drove us away, but Fritz could not know that.) Believing this, he began, as was typical of him, to think the whole thing through again, slowly and logically. He guessed that the underwater plunge through the City's outlet vents must be difficult—it would have killed me if Beanpole had not been on hand to fish me from the river—and knew the weakness of his own condition. He needed to build up strength, and the hospital offered the best chance of doing that. While he was there, he could avoid his Master's beatings and the heavy tasks that normally were laid on him. He must, of course, be careful not to arouse suspicion that he thought differently from the other slaves, which meant that he had to calculate with care the length of time he could stay. He made it last a fortnight, shamming, for the others, a weakness which increased rather than diminished as the days went by; and then, sorrowfully, declared that he realized he could no longer serve his Master as a Master should be served, and so must die. He left the hospital late in the day, heading toward the Place of Happy Release, found somewhere to hide till night fell, and then made for the Wall and freedom.

At first, all went well. He came out into the river on a dark night, swam exhaustedly to the bank, and went south, following the route we had taken. But he was a couple of days behind us, and fell further behind when a feverish chill forced him to lie for several days, sweating and starving, in a farmer's barn. He was still desperately weak when he started again, and not long after was halted by a more serious illness. This time, fortunately, he was found and looked after, for he had pneumonia and would have died without care. A lady took him in. Her son, some years before, had turned Vagrant after his Capping. She cherished Fritz because of that.

At last, when he was well and strong, he slipped away and continued his journey. He found the White Mountains swept by blizzards, and was forced to hide out near the valley villages for some time before he could make his way painfully up through deep snow. At the Tunnel, he was challenged by the single guard that Julius had left there, just in case. The guard had led him, that morning, to the caves.

All this I heard from him later. At the moment of our meeting, I merely stared, incredulous.

Julius said, "I hope you and your companion will get on together. What do you think, Will?"

Suddenly I realized I was grinning like an idiot.

Lia Kahn was perfect: rich, beautiful, popular.

Until the accident that nearly killed her.

Now she has been downloaded into a new body that only looks human.

Lia will never feel pain again, she will never age, and she can't ever truly die.

But some miracles come at a price. . . .

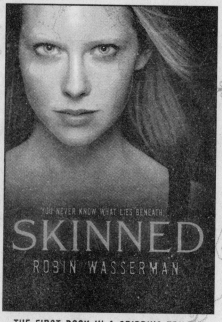

YOU NEVER KNOW WHAT LIES BENEATH.

SKINNED

ROBIN WASSERMAN

THE FIRST BOOK IN A GRIPPING TRILOGY

"A spellbinding story about loss, rebirth,
and finding out who we really are inside.
This intense and moving novel will wind up under your skin."

–SCOTT WESTERFELD

New York Times bestselling author of the Uglies series

From Simon Pulse | Published by Simon & Schuster